BLOODY HEAD

BLOODY HEAD

DANE COOLIDGE

SAGEBRUSH
Large Print Westerns

First published in Great Britain by ISIS Publishing Ltd.
First published in the United States by Dutton

Published in Large Print 2010 by ISIS Publishing Ltd.,
7 Centremead, Osney Mead, Oxford OX2 0ES
United Kingdom
by arrangement with
Golden West Literary Agency

British Library Cataloguing in Publication Data
Coolidge, Dane, 1873–1940.
 Bloody Head.
 1. Western stories.
 2. Large type books.
 I. Title
 813.5'2–dc22

ISBN 978–0–7531–8529–2 (hb)

Printed and bound in Great Britain by
T. J. International Ltd., Padstow, Cornwall

TO THE MEMORY

of

COLONEL CHARLES GOODNIGHT OF TEXAS
Who crossed the Staked Plains to the Pecos
River where, with his cattle detectives,
he ended the Lincoln County War.

CONTENTS

CHAPTER
ONE

Leopard Coat

Over the trail from the Brazos, where so many long-horned cattle had accumulated during the Civil War, a herd of steers, as trim and orderly as a Roman Legion, drifted slowly into the West. Mountain bulls rumbled defiance at them as the point headed down the old Mail Road; the horses were closely guarded against Indians and the chuck-wagon rattled along behind the herd. It was Captain Hightower's outfit, making its second drive to the Pecos.

He was taking two thousand head out of the country without so much as a "by your leave" and the Haught Family, a clan in itself, was gathered with guns in their hands. On the gallery of Henry Haught's log house, the women and children stood trembling as if the Comanches were coming; but the men-folks, armed with pistols and rifles and muzzle-loading shotguns, were down by the corrals, ready to ride.

"We're losing cattle," said Colonel Haught, "I can see that with half an eye, and Hightower is on the prod. He's a high-stomached man but the Haughts can handle him, I reckon. What say we cut his herd?"

1

"That's a dangerous thing to do, in any time and place," suggested his brother Si, "and Jack has been a Texas Ranger. But he throwed them cattle together overnight almost, and that looks bad — damned bad."

"They're stealing us blind," grumbled Long Tom Haught, resting his rifle across the horn of his saddle. "But make up your mind, boys, before you start. If he's got any in our brand, will we fight for them?"

"Till the ha'r slips," cursed big Barney Hoops; and young Ash Haught let out a yell.

"Well, come on, then!" he hollered. "What are we waiting for?"

"For orders," roared his father. "Come back hyer, you imp of Satan. There's a passel of pore white trash trailing along in the rear and we don't want to git mixed up with *them*. Never forget that the Haughts are gentlemen."

"No, sir," replied Ash, putting up his gun, and they rode out to meet the herd.

It came on in a solid line, ten feet wide and half a mile long. Two men were at the point to lead the way, two more were in the swing and two others followed behind, to shove the corners along and make way for the drag. Then letting their horses spread out to feed as they traveled, ten cowboys guarded the *remuda*. That was what the Comanches wanted — horses — and they might jump them any time.

It was ninety-six miles across the desert before they hit the Pecos River, and Indians all the way, but Jack Hightower figured it was worth it. When he came back from his first trip he had brought a mule-load of gold

— Government gold, the pay for his beef; and the sutler had ordered more. At eight cents a pound on the hoof — to feed the Reservation Navajos and the Mescalero Apaches — and all he wanted was more. For, unless they got it, the Mescaleros would go on the warpath again — and the California Volunteers were gone.

They had enlisted for the duration of the war, and the war was over. But, during the three years they had been held at Fort Sumner, they had whipped the whole Apache nation. Even given them back their arms and invited them to start all over again if they were dissatisfied with the results, but the Mescaleros acknowledged that they were whipped. These California men had a new way of fighting — the Apaches had had enough.

"You are stronger than we are," they said. "We have fought you so long as we had rifles and powder; but your arms are better than ours. Give us like weapons and turn us loose and we will fight you again."

There were eight thousand Navajos with arms in their hands and fifteen hundred Apaches, but the Indians would not fight. Regular Army soldiers were brought in — to take the places of the Volunteers — and three days after their departure the Mescaleros were gone. But they would be back with their brass tags on issue day and it behooved the new commander to have the beef. Otherwise they might attack the emigrant wagons that were going through the country to California, or kill off the Government mules.

Better than anything else the Indians loved horse-meat — they traded the cattle to the Mexicans —

3

and Captain Hightower guarded his horseherd with all a mother's care.

He had found a new market for thousands of Texas cattle, and the sight of the Government eagles had set the Brazos country aflame. He had slipped in at night, buying only longhorn steers and holding them in the corrals; and at daylight he had started for the Pecos, riding ahead in his leopard-skin vest. It was a desperate adventure, but he was playing for big stakes and he waved his cowboys on. Speed was the essence of his contract with the Government and he could not lose a day. With the Comanches he knew just what to do, but these people in the settlements were dangerous.

"Good morning, gentlemen," he said, riding to meet them, and Colonel Haught saluted him gravely.

"Good morning, sir," he responded. "Are these all your cattle?"

"Every one of them," answered Leopard Coat, indifferently.

"I doubt that!" came back Colonel Haught, and Hightower suddenly choked up.

"You doubt my word?" he thundered. "By the gods, we will see about that. Is this a cut you are trying to pull off on me? Then point out any steer, and if I can't show you the bill of sale for him I'll let you cut the whole herd."

"That yellow stag, up at the point, then. He belongs to Lem Harkins and I know it."

"His brand is CVW — I bought him myself, this morning. And what business is it of yours, or of any of your people?"

4

Hightower slammed open a sheaf of bills and pointed with a trembling finger, still waving his trail-boss on.

"I haven't got time to talk to you now," he said, "or I'd hold you accountable — personally. But tell me — is that my steer?"

"It is," replied Haught, saluting again. "I apologize — I'm very sorry. But what, may I ask, did you pay for that steer? I might offer you a few, myself."

"Eight dollars — I'm not buying. Good day, sir," answered Hightower and threw the spurs into his horse.

The mighty herd marched on, every one a full-grown steer, every one even a longhorn. For Jack Hightower had found they were a different breed of cattle — twice as strong, twice as enduring of thirst and fatigue, twice as easy to handle. It would make a difference in the trip across the desert, but he had not told the settlers.

Let them learn as he had learned, by trying. He had opened up a new market by taking big chances and now they were crazy to get in on it. Sell him their steers for any money — but two thousand head was all Hightower could handle and he was out to play a lone hand. He had a wagon crew along that he could trust — ready to fight on any occasion — and all he wanted was to be left alone.

On, on to the Concho he was pressing forward, never stopping, with the rag-tag of poor whites still behind him — but Colonel Haught did not follow.

"On your way, you damn cow thieves," he cursed, "and I hope the Comanches kill all of you. But we Haughts are gentlemen adventurers and we can play the same game, eh, Tom? Are we going to be left behind for lack of a little nerve? Let's gather every cow-brute we've got and follow this Ranger to hell. How about it, Si and Ellery, are you game to take a chance? Then back to your ranches, pack your wagons for the trail and gather every cow in your iron. Throw 'em into the corrals and meet me here tomorrow evening at sundown. Every man that's a Haught. Them that's afraid can stay behind."

CHAPTER
TWO

Indians!

Along the middle fork of the Concho, Hightower's longhorns settled down to eat the rich grass and, as darkness came on, Sam Busenback, the trail foreman, moved them out on the open ground. Every man caught up his night-horse and staked him next to his bed, but Captain Jack could not rest.

"My mule smells Injuns," he grumbled when the second guard came in. "Drive the horseherd into that gap in the brier patch yonder and double the guard outside. This is our first day out from the settlements and they're liable to start a stampede."

"Watch them steers," warned One Armed Wilson. "That mule don't smell Injuns — he smells settlers. They've been hanging on our flanks all day and they're fixing to jump the herd."

"He smells both," opined Hightower, "but the Comanches will wait for dawn. All Injuns are the same — afraid they will get killed in the dark. But these pore-whites will attack you any time."

"My mule never made a mistake yet," asserted Captain Jack. "When he snorts and fights his head there's something going to happen — right now."

There was a rumble to the north, a rush of naked horsemen against the sky line, but when the cattle jumped up the cowboys went with them. They turned to the right, ending up in a mass of horns, and chowsed around in short rushes until dawn. Then from the brier patch there came a volley of shots and the Comanches stormed down on the horse-guard. Tall Indians in war bonnets and buffalo-horn headdresses came over the brow of the hill, lances held upright and shields on their left arms, whooping like devils out of hell. Each warrior was tied to his saddle by a rope which was looped under his belt, but when Captain High-tower's buffalo-gun roared out, every Comanche dropped down out of sight.

Two horses began to pitch at the smoke-smell of the Indians; the Comanches charged in, shooting arrows; but when the six-shooters began to pop and their leading horses went down the Comanches knew they were whipped. As quickly as they had come they turned in full retreat, snatching up their wounded comrades as they fled, even throwing away their lances and shields. Then the Texans took after them, shooting to kill at close range, and not a white man's horse was lost. But the other party of "hostiles" who had hung around all night, waving blankets and giving loud war whoops, turned out to be settlers in the guise of Comanches. Only lacking the will to fight.

"Let them go," ordered Hightower, "and all hands get your breakfast as soon as the pointers start the herd. Graze them along up the stream until they get a bellyful of grass and then we'll turn off west."

He roped out a fresh horse and galloped ahead, the pointers followed along up the thin line of post oaks and the herd spread out behind. Then as the cattle, full-fed, began to lie down, the trail boss raised his hat and started them up a wash. So naturally did the herd take up the long trail that they did not know they were being driven, but it would be ninety-six miles across the desert before they drank at the Pecos. Only now the swing men rode closer, to hasten the speed of the herd.

Over the old, abandoned Stage Road the great herd moved on, following their leaders by the light of the desert stars, while the horseherd and chuck-wagon trailed behind. After their battle with the Comanches, who had lost several warriors, all danger from Indians was past, and the cowboys dozed in their saddles. With four mules to his chuck-wagon Isham Dart, the negro cook, dragged along behind the horses, passing out cups of coffee to the weary riders, who never slackened their pace. Never in all the West had there been a trail herd like this one, and, in one trip, they had got their stride.

Sixty Texas mustangs, still under heavy guard, followed along behind, just out of the dust of the herd, and never a coyote yelled but what someone listened to its cry. The hoot of an owl or the quavering wail of wolves were the favorite signals of the Comanches and Captain Hightower for one could tell the differences between the animals and their imitators. On his hardy black horse he rode in the lead till dawn, and still the great herd pressed on. It was spread out for a distance of sixty feet to escape the heat and the dust and for the longhorns there was no rest, day or night. The great thirst had come upon them, killing their desire for grass, and if they were allowed to slow down they would only pace about. Straight ahead was the only way to save them.

The heat of the summer sun beat down upon them, alkali dust rose up in clouds, and while the tired drag fell further behind the steers in the lead forged ahead. There was a mighty lowing, a bawling of anguish as the thirsty ones protested against their fate, but Captain Jack had learned from bitter experience that there could be no rest short of the Pecos. His canteens and barrels were empty of water, the pointers had to hold the leading animals back; but they had lived through it once and they could do it again. Only now Hightower turned his herd loose. They were burning up in a frenzy of thirst that only water could assuage. Down the trail which he had traveled once before, he let them set their own pace; until, just at sundown, they burst into a wild stampede. At last they could smell the dank coolness of Castle Canyon, a deep gap in the hills, but when they emerged from the other end, the river was still miles away. They had been deceived by the coolness of the rocky canyon, and there was a greater peril ahead. Out on the plain lay the sink-hole of water which had killed so many of his cows before. Five minutes after they drank the water they staggered and dropped dead, and not till many years afterward was it discovered that the lake contained arsenic. All Hightower knew was that it meant death.

Not a breath of air was stirring, apparently, but when he snatched a wisp of hair from his horse's neck and dropped it towards the ground he saw that it went northeast.

"Turn 'em south!" he yelled, holding his hat up for a signal, and the herd went pelting on. They had passed to the windward of the sunken lake when a new water-smell reached their nostrils. It came from the Pecos River, eight miles away, and already the cattle were half crazy. Across the level plains they went in a wild stampede and as the leaders reached the cut-bank of the Pecos they poured over it in a torrent, pushed on by those behind. So great was their madness that they trampled over hundreds of cattle as they passed, damming the river from bank to bank and crossing to the other side. Then, still thirsty, they turned back and plunged into the turgid stream.

Scarcely had they drunk their fill when the drag came pouring in from behind, and for a second time they piled into the alkali depths, where many of them were almost drowned. But the cowboys spurred in and pushed them down the stream, until they climbed out at Horsehead Crossing and began to graze on the wide plains. Not a steer had been lost, though many died afterwards. They had gained the Pecos again.

CHAPTER
THREE

The Haughts

The two thousand head of cattle, now feeding along the Pecos, had run the gauntlet of all the perils of the desert; but back on the Brazos there were other men as daring, and the Haughts had agreed to follow. Just home from the war, ready to brave anything to repair their shattered fortunes, the story of Captain Hightower with his mule-load of gold had driven them madly on. Knowing nothing and caring nothing for the dangers before them, every Haught went after his cows. What one man could do another could do, and the next night at sundown they were ready.

While they had been in Virginia, fighting the Yankees, this high-stomached Captain Jack had stayed at home. It was true that, while serving as a Ranger, he had never been able to draw his pay; but in fighting the Comanches, he had followed their trails to the Pecos River and discovered this cattleman's paradise. And still wearing his leopard-skin vest — which they had learned to respect — he had fought his way to Fort Sumner and come home with a pack-load of gold.

Where others had failed he had started all over again and won a princely fortune. For ten thousand dollars in gold was the acme of their dreams, and he had taken it from right under their noses. The price of beef for these starving Government Indians had been as much as sixteen cents a pound, but he had let them have it for eight. Eight cents a pound on the hoof, when all the home people got was the price of the hide and tallow, shipped down the rivers to New Orleans.

Now he had dared a second time, buying longhorns with his gold, and once more he was off to the west. Well, there were Haughts as good as any men who came up out of the West and, without listening too long to the protests of their womenfolks they struck out for the Pecos. While their neighbors — whom they hated and would have nothing to do with — slept long, after their pursuit of Hightower, the whole Haught family, with all their in-laws and children, set out on the long trail to the Pecos. Their tracks were plain and they made it into a road before the last covered wagon passed over it; but with so many cattle — cows and calves, bulls and steers — they did not get very far.

In the morning at daylight the poor-whites were upon them, demanding their right to a cut. Had not the Haughts held up Hightower and asked for his bills of sale for every steer in the herd? Then how could *they* expect to move ten thousand head of cattle without having their brands and vents inspected? Yet that was what the settlers asked, and they were willing to fight for it. Two men were shot down the first day. When they got to the Concho, their jumping-off place into the desert, it seemed as if every neighbor they had ever had was there with a gun in his hands. So they argued and harangued, while the women-folks unloaded the wagons and threw away over half the stuff.

Then it came — the stampede — and for two days and nights the Haughts were gathering up their scattered stock. They had lost hundreds of cattle, the arguments grew bitter, but no one would admit he was at fault; until on the second day Colonel Haught took command and left the women-folks standing guard. That night they held the herd with such firearms as they possessed, while the Comanches whooped like owls in the hills. And when the men came back, not a word was said, although it was generally known that eighteen men had been hung. Hung with the rawhide hobbles that every man carried, dangling around his horse's neck, but used for another purpose.

All that day the men-folks slept, shut up in the covered wagons, and not a neighbor came near to demand a belated revenge. The Haughts had struck and that night they took the trail that led off to the west. Colonel Butterfield had laid it out along the road, building stage-stands and marking out its course with white posts; but it had been moved further south, where the Indians were not so bad, and the stage-stands had been destroyed by fire. Yet it led to Horsehead Crossing where the Comanches, returning from Chihuahua, had littered the ground with the heads of horses — every one pointed towards the water.

It was there that the Indian horses drank deep — and some from the Salt Lakes sunk out of sight but strongly impregnated with arsenic. All in all, it was an eerie place of death and even the Apaches were afraid of it.

14

Yet they watched from the mountains on the other side of the Pecos, for any stray emigrants who tried to cross. The Guadelupe Mountains rose up high and very near, with great white cliffs above forests of cedars, where Indian lookouts spied on all that passed. And if any came in whose horses were not guarded, both the Apaches and Comanches swooped down on them.

If Colonel Haught understood all this it was only by hearsay, for nobody seemed to know about the West. They had seen and heard of so many signs and wonders that the telling no longer greatly interested them. All they knew was that Hightower had crossed the desert twice without leaving a dead steer on the trail. With all their books and furniture, their framed pictures and treasured heirlooms, they toiled up the middle fork of the Concho, but when they crossed over the ridge and saw the real desert, the women began to throw out their junk. Old tools, stamp irons, cracked dutch ovens and clumsy looms — for the thought of ninety-six miles without a drop of water began to make them fear the worst. But Mrs. Haught, who was a small, determined woman, still insisted on keeping her organ. She had brought it from Louisville, Kentucky, and she got off and walked. The desert stretched out before them, dim and ghostly and shrouded in mist, the dust of their passage stretched behind them; but an hour after dawn a black line appeared in the southeast and they knew it was a herd of buffalo.

They came on slowly, miles and miles of buffalo bulls on their way to their range in the north, and when their trails threatened to converge, Colonel Haught

15

rode out to turn them back. But they went on, like a great force of Nature which nothing could turn or stop; until, stampeded, they charged back through the line of cattle and scattered them to the winds. At the smell of sweating buffalos the steers threw up their heads, cows with calves and ancient bulls came to a stop. Then the long herd of cattle split squarely in the middle and let the buffalos pass through.

The ground trembled beneath the thunder of thousands of feet, half the cattle turned back toward the Brazos; while the buffalos passed close to the wagons, grunting like hogs and curling their tails. But in an hour they were gone. The drag was brought up again, the broken line re-formed, and so they went on into the night. But what they had undertaken was more than they could perform, and at daylight Colonel Haught ordered them to unhook.

"Leave your wagons," he said. "We can come back for them later. But we've got to get these cows to the Pecos or every one of them will die."

"They'll die anyhow," grumbled Barney Hoops. "Let's go back to the Concho and start another settlement."

"After what has taken place," observed Haught judicially, "I believe we'd better go on. The Brazos and the Concho are no place for us. We've got to travel light."

"But can we make it?" objected his brother Si.

"We've got to," answered Haught.

"Let us pray," interjected his wife, sinking down on her knees, and they stood silent, not wishing to interrupt. It was known that Elvina had never been quite the same since a revivalist had come to town, and when she rose up she smiled.

"The Father has told me," she said, "that our fortune lies in the West. All we need is to have faith and a way will be opened unto us."

"Very well," agreed Haught, while his relatives shrugged. "It's going to be a hard trip and any that want to can turn back. But I'm going ahead — I've got to go ahead — and Elvina has always been right."

"I *am* right," she stated. "I felt the power come over me. So ketch up your horses, take all the water you can, and never stop till you reach the Pecos."

"That's the stuff," murmured old Gram, the mother of the clan. "The Haughts have never weakened yet."

"No, and they *won't* weaken," said her son, and went out to catch up his horses.

If any horses could make it, he knew it was his thoroughbred stock. They had desert blood behind them, and Elvina took her fast mare. Then Gram caught out Selim with her own hands, while Odette and Musette both took mares. They were bright sorrels, with slim, graceful legs, high necks and glowing eyes, although nervous and hard to handle. But the daughters put on their best velvet skirts and Ash lifted them into their saddles. Then Gram mounted Selim, Elvina filled the canteens and gave each of them a sack of jerked beef.

There were others who murmured, but the Colonel Haughts had decided, and they left their covered wagons in the road. That was better than going back to the Brazos, after what they had left hanging at the gates. The settlers were the rag-tag of creation, not even good Southerners, but eighteen dead men was a little too many! And all the time the lowing cows paced on, as if realizing their destiny. They could smell the tracks of Hightower's longhorns, leading the way to the West.

CHAPTER
FOUR

"Drug!"

It was strange how Elvina's prayer had put them on the road again when all of them had been ready to quit. But the more they considered the details of what had happened that night on the Brazos, the more they were reconciled to their fate. The carpet-baggers had come in and taken over the courts and offices, there would be a harsh administration of the law, and it was only eighty miles to the Pecos, though the air was stifling hot. Great banks of black clouds were piling up in the west, the bawling of thirsty cattle had ceased, and even on the desert it might come on to rain. Had not Elvina prayed for rain?

She rode ahead with Gram, small and runty like her mother-in-law, but the two girls who followed them were thoroughbreds, like their horses, and Odette was the belle of the Brazos. She was tall, like her father, with that high-headed look so characteristic of the clan; tall and willowy, with great masses of light hair and eyes that were violet blue. A little bulging, to be sure, for the Haughts were all high-tempered; but Musette, the younger girl, had black hair and eyes, and was sweet-tempered about everything.

She rode Ona, her favorite mare, and her eyes had a faraway look, even in the waste of the desert. The wind was blowing strong now, snatching the long train of her riding skirt, which was chastely held in place by a row of leaden weights, and as the dust clouds swooped in she bowed her head against them, while her mother nodded to her encouragingly.

"Didn't the good Lord tell me," she said, "that sooner or later it would rain? I can smell the wet dust already and the damp tang of the greasewood. 'The Lord is my shepherd, I shall not want.' Even though our cattle are suffering for water I know that he will send rain."

"There! I felt a drop!" cried Gram, laughing triumphantly; and the great herd of cattle began to bawl. The rain came down in torrents striking up huge clouds of dust, which disappeared and turned instantly to mud. Then, with deafening rolls of thunder, the lightning flashed and, a moment later, it was raining hard. The bone-dry flats suddenly turned to lakes on which floated dry sticks and leaves. The cattle halted and thrust in their noses, sucking up the water and dirt.

Snatching her tin cup, Gram slid nimbly off of Selim and began dipping water into her canteen, first from the sunken circles of the ants' nests, then from the sump holes of prairie dogs. While the warm rain poured down upon them, drenching them to the skin, they filled every bottle and jug. Cattle gathered around the mud holes, drinking themselves skintight before the cowboys started them on. But half a mile further the desert turned dry again and they fell into the old Hightower trail.

It had disappeared beneath the lakes which had formed along the wayside, but now it led them on. When night came the cows began to bawl again and, just before daylight, they ran. It was the steers that took the lead for they smelled moisture in the low mountains ahead where a trail led through to the Pecos. But they passed through Castle Canyon without finding a drop of water and stampeded off across the plains. Beyond the level valley, the Guadelupe Mountains loomed up with the white skeletons of dead animals pointing west, but the steers had smelled a salt lake, sunk from sight on the prairie, and Haught's cowboys let them race.

They had lost all control of them, and they piled in over the bank of the Pecos, drinking deep from the clear water below. But they staggered as they turned back, fighting their way against the press of the herd until, weakening, they lay down and died. This was another thing the Haughts had not learned from Captain Hightower — the location of the poison lake; but when the leaders began to drop dead, Haught's cowboys charged in with a yell. Around the poisonous sinkhole they gathered in a circle, trying to push the cattle back; until, scenting the water of the Pecos, they broke into a wild stampede.

Like a waterfall, like a huge torrent, they poured over the cutbank, damming the river until it became a lake. Cattle rushed clear across, treading on the bodies of their leaders, only to turn back and plunge into the stream. It was narrow and deep but they drank it, still swimming, until at last they floated to Horsehead Crossing and spread out over the flat. There the grass grew knee-high in spite of the herds that had fed over it, but while the rest of the cows struggled to get into the salt lake Colonel Haught let these lucky ones go.

Let them charge in if they would, let them drown or swim across or run back to leap in all over again. There was a salt lake behind them whose waters were sure death, where the steers were dying by the score.

"Come on, boys," he shouted. "Let the women look after these. We've got to get back to that lake."

The men went pelting back, hardly allowing their horses to drink at the river and as they galloped across the prairie, a new peril suddenly appeared. A band of cowboys, heavily armed with rifles and pistols, rode up on the west side of the ford, and began to round up the herd.

"They are trying to steal our cattle," cried Elvina, almost in tears. "Such rough-looking men — I'm sure they're all outlaws — but I'm going to save those cows. Odette and Musette, let down your riding skirts and get back behind the walls of that stage-stand. Get every woman in there, before we're insulted, and may the Lord have mercy on our souls. It's a punishment for our sins, hanging those neighbors of ours with horse-hobbles —"

"It is not!" cried Gram vehemently, "and I won't hear you talk so. Didn't He send the rain, to keep us from dying? I'm going out to see these cowboys myself. Oh, gather your women, if you're so skeered of being insulted. There's one of them, coming down to the ford."

She whipped down to the crossing, where the river was not too deep, and waited for him to cross. He was a young man with hair almost as long as an Indian's; but he was riding a good American pony and his beard was a golden brown. He raised his hand in the peace-sign, which showed that he knew Indians, and when he splashed out he was smiling.

"Good morning," he hailed, raising his hat politely. "We just came in from Fort Davis and thought you might need help. There's a big band of Indians right up on that point, and they'll steal every cow you've got."

"No they won't," cried Elvina, riding in on him, "and you leave those cattle alone, young man. Tell your men to stop chowsing them or I'll shoot the first man I see. I'm safe in the hands of the Lord."

"All right," agreed the cowboy, beckoning in his men. "Just thought we'd help you out. You've had a bad run and your cattle are drowning —"

"All the same," cried Elvina, "they're my cows, I reckon, and I don't want them chased around. Now you get right out of here or I'll call in my husband and —"

"Never mind," said the man with the golden beard, suddenly turning mean and hard. "We're just going through and we thought you needed help. Come on, boys. Let's hit the trail."

They splashed through the ford, holding their guns up out of the water, and Mrs. Haught suddenly changed her mind. If ever eight tough outlaws were gathered together, these were the men, and half of them were laughing.

"What's the matter, Beau?" inquired a small man with a thin beard, holding up his repeating carbine. "Don't the old lady like your style? We just broke out of jail, ladies, down in Fort Davis, Jeff Davis County, but all we want is something to eat."

"You can't have it — not from me!" answered Mrs. Haught, spunkily. "Haven't we had enough trouble, with our herd stampeding and all?"

"Yes, but you can have lots more," cut in Red Ryan, laughing. "I'll jest kill that yearling and pay you for it, later. O. K., Beau?" And he raised his gun.

"Just a moment," said Beau McCutcheon, and he looked at Elvina so hard that old Gram nodded her head.

"*Bam*," went the carbine, the yearling dropped dead, and Beau took the pains to explain.

"We haven't et lately," he apologized. "Any objections if we start a fire?"

"None whatever," responded Gram promptly. "Wouldn't mind a little bite, myself. It's two days and nights since we et our last jerked beef —"

"Cut that beef up and give 'em half of it," ordered McCutcheon. "Where are all your men-folks?" he inquired and Mrs. Haught made a sign not to tell. But Gram had already begun to talk.

"They're up at the salt lake, turning cattle this way so they won't drink that water and drop dead."

"The water's poison," spoke up Red Ryan, looking up from his butchering. "Any fool ought to know that."

24

"Yes, but we're not fools," retorted Elvina, and Ryan grunted contemptuously.

"Then why don't you turn your cows down the stream," he said, "so they won't pile over the bank? Seems to me," he went on, twisting a strip of beef on a forked stick and holding it over the fire, "you're taking a good deal for granted when you call us down like that. We may not look so fancy, but we ain't cow-thieves, by a long shot. Why don't you girls come over and eat?"

He sank his teeth into the hot meat before Elvina could think up an answer, and then he knew it was a lie.

"They're not hungry," she answered faintly.

"Suit yourself," responded Ryan, as the other boys went to eating and Beau gave his first piece to Gram. Then they roasted more beef and the old lady joined in with them, but Mrs. Haught went back to the stand.

"They killed one of Hank's calves," she complained.

"Oh dear," murmured Musette, sniffing the beef. "It smells awful good to me. And who is that man with the red beard?"

"He's the one they call Beau, and he's their leader, I reckon. They've just broke jail down at Fort Davis and they're heading for the New Mexico Line. Seem to be perfectly shameless about killing our calf — I wish they'd go away."

"So do I," agreed Odette, crossly. "Why have we got to starve while they eat up our beef? I don't care. I'm going down there."

"No, you stay right here, Odette Haught," ordered her mother. "How many times have I got to tell you not to speak to men who are strangers? They are just a bunch of outlaws who have escaped from the county jail, and one of them called me an old woman."

"All the same," came back Odette, "I'm perishing from hunger and I know all you girls feel the same. So let's get our horses and lead them down there and perhaps they will give us some beef."

Without waiting for a reply she seized the reins of her mare and stepped out from behind the wall. The cowboys gazed at her appraisingly, one or two raised their hats, and Odette came right to the point.

"Boys," she said, "I'm simply perishing from hunger, no matter what my mother says. Will one of you gentlemen kindly give me a piece of beef, or will I have to take it?"

She looked very trim and statuesque in her long velvet gown and, five minutes later, she was sitting down beside Gram and eating a piece of meat. All the other girls followed suit, the sullen Ryan was all smiles, and in half an hour's time the whole Haught family was breaking its long fast, although Elvina would not eat. Gram passed her up a piece, she went off by herself and from a broken-down wall she mounted her thoroughbred mare, sitting up in her saddle like an aristocrat.

They saw at a glance then that these were quality-folks and rose in a body to offer help, but the fair Odette strode over and swung up without assistance. Musette followed, the whole Haught family mounted and, hooking up their skirts — which hung two feet from the ground — they felt that all danger was past. Not a cowboy had got fresh or offered any unwanted attentions in the brief time they had been gnawing at the meat, but Elvina was adamant in her disapproval and led them off at a lope.

Now that Red Ryan had mentioned it, there was no use drowning good cows. The thing to do was to turn them down the river and let them drink at the ford. She even let a couple of the boys cross over and bring in the herd from the west. All was suddenly good will, as if nothing had happened, but the golden-bearded McCutcheon did not mount. There was a hereafter coming for this when the Haught men came riding back and saw who was squiring their dames. He sat down in the shade of the old adobe wall, and took out a little book.

Then it happened — so quick that no man could stop her. The mare Ona almost stepped on a rattlesnake. She jumped back and jumped again, tripped and fell and leapt up a second time, and Musette went over backwards. It was all due to the velvet skirt, hanging two feet below her feet, and Musette snatched for the horn, but missed. The mare started running, kicking back at the dragging woman, bucking wildly, then kicked again. Two men shook out their loops, made a throw and missed. It often happened in those days of long skirts and women's saddles, not built for safety.

The cowboys dashed after her, trying to build a new loop, but Musette was down and being "drug." One chance was left and Beau McCutcheon took it. He shot the beautiful mare — twice. The first time he missed her, but the second time she dropped dead, with Musette's foot still tangled in the stirrup. He rushed in and caught her up again, releasing the little boot, and carried her back to the shade. As she lay limp in his arms he laid her down and began to manipulate her ankle — and then a fury struck him.

"Get away from her," cried Elvina, jerking down the mass of skirts. "What do you mean by such impertinence? I'll give you to understand, sir, that my daughter is a lady. You've killed her horse. That's enough."

Beau McCutcheon stepped back, dazed, but he waited until he saw Musette stir. Then he mounted and rode away.

CHAPTER
FIVE

The Hightower
Horseherd

One after the other the cowboys dashed after their leader as he took the trail up the river, but he was riding like the wind.

"Damn a woman," he muttered. "The old heifer struck me when I was trying to help her girl. I wouldn't hurt Musette for anything in the world. She was such a sweet little thing."

"Never mind, boy," said Montague Payne, catching up with him. "The old lady was out of her mind. If you hadn't killed that mare she would have drug Musette to death. But seems like we get in wrong everywhere."

Payne was a wanderer, another college boy gone wrong, and he spurred close up beside McCutcheon.

"The boys looked a little rough," he commented. "But they didn't mean any harm. She was a beautiful little girl — and they all tried to ketch the mare — but if you hadn't shot it, she'd be dead."

"Sure as hell," nodded Beau. "I tried to crease the mare the first time. But she was crazy — I had to kill her. And then Musette's mother gave me a slap in the face and told me to get away."

"The whole bunch was kind of nuts," laughed Red Ryan, riding up. "Do you know what she did when Odette raised her veil? Reached over and pulled it down!"

"But Musette is just a child," complained Beau. "She's hardly got her growth. And when I tried to help her —"

"The old lady hit you," ended Red Ryan. "She was that way from the start. But when I looked up at her and said: 'Any fool ought to know that,' she knowed that I meant *her*.

"'Why don't your girls come over and eat?' I asked, intending to get acquainted.

"'Because they're not hungry,' she said. And then that Odette girl walked right down past her and asked for something to eat. 'I'm simply perishing from hunger,' she said. 'Will one of you gentlemen please give me a piece of beef, or have I got to steal it?' How's that for nerve? And I handed over a chunk of meat, stick and all. You ought to see the smile she gave me."

"Well, we're all dished now," answered Beau McCutcheon bitterly, "with that old hen running the roost. Right away, when I asked her if we couldn't be some help, she decided we were stealing her cattle, and if the Texas Rangers should show up she'd send them on our trail, damned quick."

"She'd tell 'em right where to find us," laughed Red Ryan. "In the first saloon, getting drunk."

"Say, there's a big bunch of cattle up ahead of us," said McCutcheon. "The tracks were made today, and, following along behind them, are some barefooted pony tracks — bunch of Comanches, out to steal their horses, I reckon. Sure as hell, when they pass the point of Guadelupe Mountain, they'll jump 'em."

"I can see the cattle's dust," exclaimed Red Ryan, "and it's coming on to storm. Maybe this is that Captain Hightower that Odette was telling about; and sa-ay, boys, was she a pretty girl!"

"Never mind the girl," interrupted Beau. "What did she say about Hightower? We might speed up and throw in with his outfit, along about eating time."

"You said it," responded Ryan, jumping his horse into a lope.

"I used to know Captain Hightower, when he was a Ranger. He's bringing two thousand head of cattle across the desert to deliver them at Fort Sumner. If we can get in with him we might begin to eat regular again. That would be a good job for all of us, and he's got a swell nigger cook.

"Right up ahead there," went on Ryan, "is where New Mexico begins. You might be interested, Mr. McCutcheon, in case the Texas Rangers show up. Because the man that owns that horse you're riding is going to be coming after him."

"Sure is," agreed Beau. "But I didn't steal this bay — just took the wrong horse by mistake. Feeling around in the nighttime —"

"Yes," laughed Bobbie Skeets. "But I noticed you got a good one. Best pony in the corral."

31

"Well, I did," protested McCutcheon. "Best horse I ever rode, though, and sure as hell somebody will come after him. I'm going to keep a-going until I get to California, and then I'll be looking backwards."

"You've been looking over your shoulder," jested Ryan, "ever since we rode out of Fort Davis. But the line is right ahead here, if you can see the monument, and when we get across, we're safe. I came down through this country two years ago —"

"It's raining," announced Skeets, as a rattle of big drops hit in on them; and then he began to sing.

"Out with the herd and coming on to rain
And my damned old slicker is back in the wagon."

The black clouds piled up as they had been doing for several days, dragging long trailers across the sky, flooding one place and missing all the rest; but a blinding flash of lightning appeared in the north and they went up the trail at a lope. A big storm swept down upon them, obscuring the view, and they knew that Hightower was not far away. In the distance they could hear the bellowing of cattle, and then suddenly a wild stampede.

When Indians were near, although keeping out of sight, the steers would dash away from them, repelled by the rank odor of smoke. Now, from the banks of the Pecos, where they had been hiding in some wash, a party of Comanches, glamorous in war-bonnets and buffalo heads, rode in recklessly, following after the

32

rush. Then, shying away from the cowboys, they turned and swung back on the horse-herd.

That was what they had come for — the horses — and while the Texans were riding after the cattle they rushed them past the wagon and headed down the trail. Along the river, every man waving a blanket or brandishing his lance in the air, they bore down like a whirlwind on the astonished cowboys, who were riding the other way. But Beau McCutcheon and his men had been raised on the Border since they were boys, and they knew it was Hightower's horseherd.

The Comanches were heading for Pope's Crossing — where the banks of the river were low — but all eight cowboys drew their pistols and charged. Regardless of numbers, every man for himself, these sons of old Texas lived up to their traditions and whirled in on them from the rear. The horseherd was crossing the river, and that slowed the Indians down. Then suddenly the Comanches turned back on them. But when the pistols began to pop and naked Indians to go down they halted and put up a fight.

There were fifty or sixty Indians, armed with lances and shields and some with old-fashioned pistols, but the Texans rode right into them, shooting their Navy six-shooters with both hands, but keeping right on. That was the only way they knew, and on his black-maned bay Beau McCutcheon took the lead. A Comanche warrior rode out at him, horse and man went down; then, with bows and arrows and lances, the Indians closed in on him. A chief seized his war club, swung it by the horse-tail at the end and hurled it into the crowd.

Something hit Beau on the head as he was fighting in the melee and he tumbled off under his horse's feet. The next thing he knew there were Texans all around him and a bearded man was examining his head.

"He'll live," he said, whipping out a white rag and wrapping it around the cowboy's bloody locks. "You can't hurt a cowboy in the haid. Bring those horses back, men, before someone else jumps us. You did well, boy — charged right into them. I saw you from behind."

CHAPTER
SIX

Warriors

"Is this your horse?" inquired Hightower, coming back with Beau's bay, "A good animal, boy. Bay, with a black mane and tail. A true mustang, the strongest breed there is. Seems to me I've seen that horse before, somewhere."

"You might have," admitted McCutcheon, sitting up and feeling of his head. "He belongs to a Texas Ranger named Rye Miles."

"From Fort Davis? He belonged to my company."

"Best horse I ever had," said Beau. "Well-reined — never gets tired — with a walking trot that's hard to beat. But I expect Mr. Miles to be coming after him. Although I left a good roan in his place."

"*Oh* — oh!" grunted Hightower. "Traded horses, eh — by mistake?"

He straightened up and shouted orders to take the horseherd back, but McCutcheon did not let the matter drop.

"Yes," he said. "We left there in the nighttime and took the first animals we could find. It was what you might call a forced play, with the Rangers and deputy sheriffs both after us. But we're across the line in New Mexico now, so I reckon old Hot Foot is mine."

"Maybe so and maybe not," observed Hightower. "I happen to know this man Miles and he thinks a lot of his horse. However, Mr. — er —"

"McCutcheon," put in Beau promptly. "Beauregard McCutcheon, from Waxahatchie, Texas."

"Well, Mr. McCutcheon," went on Hightower, "I'm glad to make your acquaintance. Especially under the circumstances — turning my horseherd back for me and all that. Mighty clever of you boys to go to so much trouble to help an absolute stranger, and if I can speak a good word for you don't hesitate to mention it. About those Rangers, you know. The finest remedy for that head of yours is a poultice of prickly pears, and if you can ride your horse until we get into camp I'll guarantee to fix it up. None of your friends got hurt, I'm glad to say, but if you come from Waxahatchie you must be related to an old friend of mine, Joe McCutcheon. He was a first-class fighting man, but the Comanches finally got him."

"He was my uncle," explained Beau. "My father was killed two years ago."

"Oh! Too bad. And what was his name?"

"Beauregard Ismay McCutcheon."

"Yes, yes. An honorable name, but I don't happen to recognize it. Was he in the Rangers, too?"

"Yes, sir. With Captain Jack Cureton."

"Well, well!" exclaimed Hightower, helping him up on his horse. "I was a scout for old Jack, myself, once. But we'd better keep up with the horseherd or the

Indians might jump us again. They hang around the point of Guadelupe Mountain and we can always count on their attacking us somewhere. But since we've got these Navy pistols they're getting kind of shy. I've fought quite a number of Indians in my day and there's one thing I've found out. There are very few of them that will stand up to gunpowder, and your boys have all learned to shoot. Of course the Comanches always carry off their wounded, but you winged quite a few of them, I reckon."

"I knocked down two," said Beau, "but something hit me on the back of the head and —"

"That was a war club," grinned Captain Jack. "The Comanches tie a cow-tail on the end of the handle and throw it like a sling. I happened to shoot that *hombre* right after he hit you, but you've certainly got a sore head. You'll have to be my guest while I poultice you up and give you a few square meals. I've got the finest cook in the country — his name is Isham Dart. He's always got beans and beef and coffee, and what more does a man want? I'm taking two thousand head of steers to Fort Sumner, but we'll stop at Deep Lake first. And by the way, you tell your friends to stop at my wagon and Isham will feed them good."

"I'll do that, and I thank you; but we killed a beef down at Horsehead Crossing and —"

"A *beef!*" yapped Hightower. "Did you happen to find a stray?"

"No, there's about ten thousand head more down there and —"

37

"Who do they belong to?" cursed the Captain. "Why, we just left the Crossing yesterday, and all I saw was ten thousand *rattlesnakes*."

"The cattle had crowded in until they dammed the whole stream. Belonged to a man named Haught."

"Hell's bells, is he there already? He's rushing in to spoil my market! Excuse me, Mr. McCutcheon, but this is very important. I knew these settlers would follow after me."

He spurred off, grumbling into his beard, and when Beau caught up he was waving his hat and urging the point men on.

"Was that Henry Haught?" he asked, coming back.

"Henry or Hank or call him what you will. When we came to the crossing there were about forty women and not a single man. They were all up at a salt lake, where their cows were dying by the hundred, and when I crossed the ford the women took us for cattle-thieves, and ordered us on our way. So we turned the cows loose and swam across to the other side and Red Ryan killed a yearling without hardly asking permission and we all began to eat.

"The old lady, who was doing most of the talking, herded the other women into the stage-stand, but a fine-looking girl caught her horse and came down and they all began to eat broiled meat. That was the end of it, as far as I was concerned. I lay down in the shade, but while I was reading a book one of their horses stepped on a rattlesnake and pretty near killed a girl, running away.

"Well, I shot her horse when it passed, and the next thing I knew a woman slapped me over, giving me hell and telling me to be on my way. We were coming up on the trail when we ran into those Comanches, and all the time we never saw a Haught. But that old lady was sure on the warpath —"

"She sent us away like she owned the country," complained Red Ryan; and Jack Hightower grunted scornfully.

"How the hell they crossed that desert," he said, "is more than I can understand. But one thing is certain — they're going to spoil our market unless we push this herd right through."

He held up his sombrero and waved it at those in front, and came back talking to himself.

"Mr. McCutcheon," he began, "and all you gentlemen who so kindly turned back our horseherd, we thank you from the bottom of our hearts and I want you to eat at the wagon. My pardner, Martin Hockaday, has got a ranch up above here, and I won't rest, day or night, until we make this delivery. You look like good cowmen and he'll probably have a job for you. Isham, give these men some grub."

"Yes, suh, and thank you, suh," answered a voice from the chuck-wagon. "Jest ride up close, gentlemen, and I'll pass out the best I've got."

A small, black colored man, driving a team of four mules, looked up at them with a beaming smile and, while they drank their coffee and ate some corn bread and beans, he kept on along the road.

"The Captain, suh," he explained to Beau, "is mighty proud of this mess-wagon of his, the first of its kind in the world. Done invented it hisself, without any assistance. Now all the other outfits is making some. Whenever I stop I build a little fire with some buffalo chips I carry along under the wagon in a big piece of tarp I've got. I prepare my dinner while the men are eating breakfast, and I always keep my coffee hot. Yes, suh, and thank you, suh, always glad to make you welcome. Heah's some pine pitch that will be good for that wounded head of yours. Yes, suh, if all the boys would fight Injuns the way you do there wouldn't be a Comanche on the trail. But when they doubled back and stole our horses I shuah expected to be scalped."

Isham laughed as he handed them out some light bread and molasses, but all through the night Hightower's longhorns went tramping on, for Haught had given him a scare. If a party of women and children, with ten thousand head of mixed cattle, could come across the desert like that, it would not be long before others would follow. Every cowman would hit the trail.

They crossed the Pecos at daylight on to a broad and level plain, with here and there a small bunch of cattle, but they were mostly cows with calves, not half of which bore brands. It was a virgin cow-country, with salt-grass and grama, and a few cotton-woods along the stream. A beautiful country, much preyed upon by the Comanches who stole the cattle and traded them to the Mexicans. It was horse-meat they were after, preferring it to beef, and Hockaday had let them steal. That was easier than keeping up a constant warfare, and Martin was always short-handed.

He was a tall, lanky man, mounted on an old potbellied mare, with a rope hackamore and a boy's kak saddle — not the kind of man you would expect to find as king of all that country. But, over all those wide plains, as far as a man could see, he ruled by the force of his powerful personality and the magnetism of his smile. He lived at Deep Lake in the middle of the valley, where the herds all stopped for water, and as Hightower's men crossed the river he rode down the trail to meet them.

"What's this I hear?" he asked as he shook hands with Captain Hightower, "about ten thousand head of cattle, coming clear across the desert, with a mixed herd, and bulls and everything?"

"It's Henry Haught, from the Brazos," answered Hightower. "And if I don't deliver these steers right away I'll lose a right smart of money. It rained when he was halfway across the desert or he'd have lost every cow he had."

"Sho, sho, Jack," commented Hockaday. "It just shows the age of miracles ain't past. My two nephews, John and Lester, are over on the Brazos now, picking up two more herds."

"I tell you, Martin," yelled Hightower, "people don't know how bad these Indians are. I happened to get by the first time, because I'd followed the buffaloes south, but they're coming north a million strong, with all the Comanches in the country behind them. Are those the cattle you contracted to give me for a dollar a head, over the market? Then I warn you, right now, send some men out to help those boys or they'll lose every cow they've got."

"Don't think so," laughed Hockaday. "The Comanches are too busy roasting buffalo humps and cutting out the tongues. These cows will be all right to sell to the Government to feed to the Reservation Navajos, but the Mescaleros wouldn't touch 'em. Too tough. They'd rather have horse-meat."

"Yes, there you are again," retorted Captain Jack. "What's to keep 'em from running off your horseherd? Only yesterday they jumped ours, right in the middle of a big stampede, and if these boys hadn't happened to be following along behind me and put up a hell of a good battle, I believe I'd be following them yet. You see this man here, with his head wrapped up in a rag? He got that from a blow with a war club that mighty nigh cracked his skull open."

"Well, well," commented Hockaday, looking closer. "So he put up quite a battle, hey? I could use a few men like that to guard my lower range. Those twenty-three cowboys that I've been feeding all winter, doing nothing but running up bar-bills, pulled out on me last week, taking half their horses with them, and went up the trail to Denver."

"Well, in that case," said Hightower, "I've got just what you're looking for, Martin. Eight of the fightingest warriors that ever came up the trail. Shake hands with Mr. McCutcheon, of Waxahatchie, Texas. Just come up from Fort Davis. They might take on with you for a while."

42

"Well, Jack," chuckled Hockaday, "this is sure providential, like that rainstorm that saved Henry Haught. I need a few good, nervy men, to cut these herds when they come through. Forty dollars a month, no work to do, and all the whisky you can drink."

"Sure!" agreed Bobbie Sheets, laughing.

"Going to cut Henry Haught's herd?" inquired Red Ryan, "then put me down on your book right now. His wife called us cow-thieves the minute she seen us, and I don't like the old heifer, nohow."

"Hired!" nodded Hockaday. "How about you, young man?"

He turned to Beau McCutcheon, who shook his sore head and laughed.

"Nope," he said. "Little out of my line, cutting trail-herds. I'm just going through on my way to California, but I thank you, just the same."

"Well, stay around a while," invited Hockaday, hospitably, "and let your head heal up. Jest the sight of that white rag is all you really need, if you got it fighting the Comanches."

"He did that!" spoke up Hightower. "I was there and saw him do it. He got that head in a battle with the chief; and, young man, let me tell you something. Next time you go after them you wear that bloody rag, the way I wear this Leopard Coat. They'll call you Bloody Head or something like that, and look up to you, like a warrior."

"All right, call me Bloody Head," answered Beau. "But I'm on my way to California. These boys can stay if they want to —"

"Yes," observed Red Ryan, grinning. "The fact is, Mr. Hockaday, Beau done stole a Ranger's horse and he wants to get away with it."

"Oh, that's all right," laughed Martin. "I don't care who owns a horse, as long as I get to ride it. And I don't care who owns a cow as long as I brand the calf. My hands have quit so often that half my cattle are mavericks —"

"I didn't steal that horse," denied Beau hotly. "I just traded for him in the dark, leaving a damned good roan in his place. But my old man brought me up never to brand a neighbor's cow and I haven't got over it, yet."

"That's right, son," nodded Hightower, approvingly. "I swear half the cows on the Brazos are wearing some other man's brand. I paid the top price, had 'em give me a bill of sale and even then I nearly had a cut. This same Henry Haught that's coming over to ruin my market rode out and tried to stop me. But that's something I've never submitted to yet; and I warn you, Martin Hockaday, I want a good bill-of-sale for every cow those nephews of yours bring in."

"Aw, sho, sho, Jack," laughed Hockaday. "Did I ever sell you a cow that didn't have a straight brand? But I can't hire cowboys to brand up my mavericks, so I wait until I make a sale and slap on the road-brand, right then!"

"All right, if that's the way you work it," grumbled Hightower. "You're the first man that fetched she-stuff into the country and it stands to reason the mavericks are yours. But over on the Brazos there's men who make a business of branding up *orehannos*."

"Haven't hardly been worth stealing," shrugged Hockaday. "And I just cain't keep these warriors. I hired a bunch of Mexicans to do the work and they wouldn't get mounted till noon. Horses like I've got, it takes a man to handle 'em."

"We'll ride 'em," promised Red Ryan; and Hockaday hired them all. Except one.

CHAPTER
SEVEN

Sound Principles

"So you're going to cut the Haught herd," observed Ryan with a shrug. "Well, that's where I shine — cutting trail-herds."

"Coming in and going out, at the other edge of my range," sighed Hockaday. "Got to do it or they'll run off all my cattle. 'Cut 'em down to the trail-brand,' that's my motto. I have to protect myself, somehow."

"Fair enough," agreed Red, "and we'll start in on Henry Haught. His wife as much as told us we were a bunch of common cow-thieves, and I don't like the old heifer, nohow. But she's got a daughter I'd sure like to put my iron on. That girl, Odette. Eh, Jim?"

"Prettiest girl I ever saw," nodded Harry, as they rode along beside the wagon. "Jest as slim and straight, and with all that blonde hair. But hard to put your hand on, I reckon."

"That's where I shine, again," boasted Ryan. "Making up to these pretty girls. But the old lady has got us down in her black books, on account of Beau shooting that mare."

"I had to do it," defended McCutcheon, "or she'd have been drug to death, right there. And I'll thank you boys not to mention the subject again. What did you want me to do — let her get killed?"

"No!" spoke up Jim Brady, "you did just right, Beau. Our reatas were so stiff from getting rained on that we couldn't rope a short-horn. But you were out ahead, you saw us both miss and you killed the mare, like *that!*"

He snapped his fingers, but Beau turned away and for a long time he rode in silence. Then he fetched a book out of his war bag and read it as he passed along. It was a copy of *Romeo and Juliet* — the boys called him Shakespeare George — but that was just the name for another man they had known before they were locked up in jail. It had been a forced play, with the Rangers fighting against the sheriff and a big gang of outlaws horning in; but, with Jeff-Davis County bankrupt and the judges afraid to officiate, Beau McCutcheon had broken out of jail.

They had all broken out together, taking back their guns and saddles and grabbing the first horses they could find; and, even across the line, Beau McCutcheon still glanced backward and muttered to himself. Where the sheriff hadn't been paid and caravan robbers ran the country, six months was long enough for any man to wait trial, in a court that never convened.

The Rangers had arrested them, following a fight in a saloon, but there had been no one to turn them loose again. All the judges had resigned, being afraid to pronounce judgment against the bandits and, as the summer came on, the snake-hole had begun to get hot. It was a pitch-black hole, blasted out of the solid rock and covered with enormous timbers, but Beau McCutcheon had put his back against one and let every prisoner out.

They had recovered their saddles, their guns and their rigging — and all that would have been forgiven them — but when they rode off on the first horses they could find they had committed the unpardonable sin. For those horses belonged to the Texas Rangers and it had put six men afoot.

Deep Lake appeared before them, a circle of blue water on the prairie, where cattle continually came and went, and cottonwoods grew along the ravine. It welled up from the plain, a huge artesian spring, ten acres across, flowing away towards the river in a wooded ravine, from which the water had been diverted to Martin's ditch. It was the boast of Hockaday that he could sit on his back porch and catch fish from the rushing stream. The old fort was a bunk-house where any man could sleep, and he welcomed them all to his table.

"Make yourselves at home, boys," he said to the grinning cowboys. "The barroom is right over there, and for these men I've just hired I've got something special — a brand-new bullpen, just finished and fully furnished. Want to see it? Well, come on in, then."

He led the way to a square adobe structure, and bowed to them as he opened the door. The bullpen was empty, even having a dirt floor, but in each corner there stood a full bottle of whisky, with another one in the middle for luck. This was their introduction to the Long Rail brand, where for several years he had hired all who came, without ever having enough men. His last aggregation, a gang of thirty men, had left him in a body, hiring out for double his wages and leaving their bar-bills unpaid.

The new men took a drink all around, to celebrate finding such a kind master; but Beau McCutcheon camped under a tree, for the wound on his head was bad. There was no prickly-pear cactus on those barren plains from which a poultice could be made, and Isham Dart's pine pitch did not seem to be very efficacious. So he lay down in the shade and let the world go by, for Hightower had to hurry on.

Yet before Hightower left — to deliver his long-horned steers before Colonel Haught rode in on him — Captain Jack found time to make him a visit.

"Mr. McCutcheon," he said, "if it wasn't for you I'd be chasing Comanches, this minute, and maybe losing my horseherd. Now I want you to look my horses over as they pass by and pick out the best animal you can find."

"Many thanks," answered Beau, rousing up. "And if you've got another mustang half as good as the horse I stole I'll try to send old Hot Foot back. Best horse I ever rode, but he really belongs to Rye Miles."

"Yes, he does," agreed Hightower, "and I'll tell you, Mr. McCutcheon, I don't think you'll ever regret this. Because Rye Miles is a fighting fool when it comes to losing his mount. So I'll pick out another bay with a black mane and tail and you'll never know the difference. And the first man I can trust that is going down that way I'll send back old Hot Foot, personally.

Your father was right when he brought you up never to lie or steal, or brand another man's cattle. I never hire a man like that myself, and Martin Hockaday may live to regret it.

"Now I've got to be pushing on, to deliver these longhorn cattle, but I'm going to remember you as a man of sound principles. Don't fail to look me up if you happen to be passing my way. I can use a man like you."

CHAPTER
EIGHT

Romeo and Juliet

It was five days later, Hightower had delivered his long-horned steers and was heading back to Texas for more, when the first herd of Henry Haught's cattle appeared on the lower range. They traveled as always in straggling bunches, each man with his brand separate from the rest, the covered wagons following behind. They had lost over two thousand head, out on the desert and from drinking poisonous water, but they came on in a body, the steers in the lead, the cows and calves strung out behind.

Martin Hockaday loped down to meet them, expecting to find his two nephews, and when he heard that their herds had been stampeded he gave way to a fit of cursing. It had been Lester's fault, for he had let his cows get strung out and the Indians had rushed in upon them. Eleven hundred head of cattle had gone like the wind and then the Comanches had come back for the horses. Not satisfied with the buffaloes which were still moving north, they had charged in and run off the horseherd, and when Hockaday heard the news he wheeled his old mare and galloped back to Deep Lake.

"Mr. McCutcheon," he complained, "I've got two of the orneryist nephews that the good Lord ever let live. They're my sister's sons and I try to put up with them, but neither one has got a lick of sense. Here Jack Hightower has crossed that desert twice without ever losing a cow, and these boys have let their whole herd be stampeded; and lost all their horses, to boot. And here this Haught outfit, with all their women and children and ten thousand head of mixed cattle, come through without losing a cow. That is, until they reached the river and drank that pisen water at the lakes. I hear they lost two thousand head."

He went off talking to himself while the Haught herd moved slowly on, and when Lester and John came in to report he sent them back for more.

"Go back and get those cattle," he stormed. "Grab the first eleven hundred you can ketch and put them on the trail. Your uncle is under contract to deliver them to Jack Hightower and he won't take no for an answer. Look at these Haughts, bringing in that many cattle and fixing to bust our market. Herding their cows with women on horseback, riding around with long-tailed skirts. I'll hold 'em while you gather your cowboys — then I want you to go back. Understand?"

The first of the Haught herds moved in slowly, spreading out around the lake as they watered, then drifting out to graze. They were a hard-looking outfit, after going back for their wagons and hauling them down to the Pecos; and in the midst of their watering a caravan of Gospel Healers came toiling in from the north. But Hockaday made them welcome. In all that land, for two hundred miles, his was the only spring of water free from alkali and, while eight thousand head was a pretty large order, he had his reasons for inviting the Haughts to stay.

"Why, yes," he said as he met the Haught womenfolks — who had taken him for the hired man. "There's plenty of room for all. That's what I need, is good neighbors. Just turn your cattle loose and it won't cost you a cent to gather them. My boys will bring them in on the regular roundup. Glad to do it, to have someone to dance with."

He laughed so wholeheartedly that Mrs. Haught insisted upon making camp; but Henry Haught had had trouble with his neighbors before this and he ordered his cows close-herded. It was forty miles from the cliffs of the Staked Plains to the high mountains on the west; and from Fort Summer, where the Indians were kept, to the Texas line, it was nearly two hundred miles more. But the Haughts were glad to stop where the grass was so rank and high, and the Indians were kept away.

"Injuns?" repeated Martin Hockaday. "With those soldiers right up here, not forty miles away? I've had my horses stolen more times than you can count, but a few neighbors will fix all that. The Government feeds the rascals and pays us for the beef, so we're glad to have 'em stay. There's ten thousand Navvies and fifteen hundred Apaches. The sutler comes down here and buys our cattle for eight cents a pound on the hoof. Have you got a few fat steers you'd like to sell? Or some that are not so fat? You'll have to look out, though, or the Comanches will steal your horses. You can put them in my corral, if you like."

It seemed to Henry Haught almost too good to be true, after some experiences he had had, and he put double guards over his horseherd. But that very night someone stampeded half his cattle and he drove his horses into the corral. Then, right in the middle of this good fortune, Haught met a man he knew: Captain Jack Hightower, with twenty-five good men, returning to the Brazos for more beef.

"Mr. Hightower," he said, riding out to meet him. "I understand you're buying beef."

"I am," returned Captain Jack, "but only from my friends, and I don't include you in that class. You tried to cut my herd when I was over on the Brazos, and that's something I never forget."

He spurred his horse ahead, his cowboys scowling back at the Haughts, and the Haught boys knew they were ditched. In fact, they were beginning to have a hunch that certain news had preceded them; of eighteen neighbors, hung by the neck with horse-hobbles — and the Hightower cowboys looked death. Even the seven men who rode the range for Hockaday had suddenly changed their ways. Down at Horsehead Crossing they had been more than gallant — after the ladies had accepted their broiled beef — but when Mrs. Haught had ordered them away they had taken great offense. And now, over the line in New Mexico, the jail-breakers from Fort Davis, who had been fleeing from the Texas Rangers, were discovered in a position of authority. They were Martin Hockaday's "warriors," hired to fight for his rights, and even the beauteous Odette was disregarded. Instead of getting up a dance, where they could continue their harmless flirtations, the cowboys still referred to Mrs. Haught as an old heifer and kept away from her entirely. Red Ryan had called her a fool to her face and Haught had intended to rebuke him, but Red was so obviously on the prod that he wisely refrained from antagonizing him.

Beau McCutcheon, about whom nothing was said, had been the leader of their band and in his absence the women could learn nothing, except from the Mexicans who worked about the place. He was ill, they learned that — struck down by a war club in the hands of a Comanche warrior, who had been killed the next minute by Hightower. But when Mrs. Haught had ordered Beau away — after he had saved her daughter from certain death — she had alienated the good will of every warrior on the rancho. Even the Mexican rancheros agreed that Don Beau was *muy hombre*, one man in a hundred when it came to fighting Indians. But he had been injured — they would say no more.

The Haught clan had camped not far from the ditch which drained off the waters from the lake. A long ditch, full of running water and shaded by rank-growing cottonwoods, under one of which McCutcheon had taken refuge. While Red Ryan and the rest had moved into the new bullpen and celebrated by a general carouse, Beau had camped outside under a brush *ramada* and sunk into a moody silence. If there were Haughts up the ditch, or even passing down it, he did not want to see them, but the mystery of his hiding-place was finally solved by old Gram, who gave a Mexican two-bits.

Beau was lying face-down on a pile of prairie grass when a skinny hand reached over and touched him, but when he looked up and saw who it was he did not even smile. Gram was all right and the head of the clan but he had formed a low opinion of the Haughts. They were like any other Texas clan, composed of all kinds, good and bad; and if the men were like the women he did not want to have anything to do with them. But Gram stepped over the plank which had been laid across the ditch and placed a hot cookie in his hand.

"That was sent to you," she said, "by one who wishes you well and would like very much to see you. She herself has been sick, having been drug by a horse, but she asked me to come and see you."

"Oh!" exclaimed McCutcheon, and smiled. Then he ate the hot cookie which had been baked for him and turned his face away.

"And will you come with her?" he asked.

"Just as you please. She is my dearest granddaughter and I would not wish any harm to come to her. At the same time she is so sweet —"

"Then come with her," he said, and shut his eyes.

At last she had found him, this Musette that he had dreamed about but had never expected to see again. He had watched for her through the stakes that served for a barricade and kept people from looking in as they passed; but he was glad that at last she had found him, although his head was still bad. It ached and throbbed in a most disconcerting way and the cowboys all suggested new remedies. But here was one who could cure him, merely by her presence.

He was lying just as Gram had left him when she rode up on a dish-faced little Indian pony and, when she did not get off he knew that she had been hurt. Badly hurt, though she still wore her long velvet riding-habit, hanging two feet from the ground.

"Let me lift you off," he cried, leaping up, and Gram held her horse's head. Then he reached up reverently and took her from the saddle that had so nearly caused her death. She was lighter than he had thought for, and her face was pale, but when he put her down she lifted up her lips and kissed him.

"I had to thank you," she said, "for all you have done. There is a revivalist in town and Mother does not know. She is down there singing glory hallelujah."

She smiled, with a trace of bitterness, and Gram sat down outside, holding their two horses, saying nothing.

"I do not agree with her about everything," Musette went on, sinking down on a heap of hay. "But Grandma has told me it will be all right to see you, as long as she is along."

"Or even if she wasn't," answered Beau, moving over beside her. "I have wanted to see you, to find out how badly you are hurt, and to speak to you about that skirt. It is a very pretty skirt but dangerous for you to wear. I hated to kill your horse but I had to do it. The Indian women don't wear long skirts."

"I know it," she replied, blushing a rosy red and brushing the hair out of her eyes. "But — oh, Mr.

57

McCutcheon, if you knew how I hate them! I want to ride free, like men!"

"Then do it," he advised. "Get one of these buckskin suits, such as the Indian women always wear. They come halfway below the knees and —"

"But Mother will never let me do it," she sighed. "Let's talk about something else. This is the second time I've been drug from the saddle and it came near being my last."

"It did that," he agreed. "I was shooting at two hundred feet and your mare was pitching and running. But of course, if your mother objects —"

"*I* don't!" spoke up the harsh voice of Gram, "I've been thrown a hundred times, and every time I believed it was my last. Why women wear such skirts is more than I can imagine, but some French queen was born deformed and she *had* to wear one, and all the others had to follow suit. It was anything to be in the style. Are you a book-reader, Mr. McCutcheon? What is that book you have there?"

"Oh, it's *Romeo and Juliet*, by Shakespeare — you've heard of it, I'm sure."

"Yes, I've heard of it," admitted the old lady. "But somehow I've never read it. In the Girls' Seminary which I attended back in Louisville, it wasn't considered very nice."

"Perhaps not," responded Beau, tucking it under his coat. "But while I've been lying here with no one to talk to —"

"Let *me* read it," begged Musette, reaching out.

58

"Your mother might think it would ruin your morals," he said. "They spoke a different language in those days, and called a spade a spade."

"Oh, let me have it," she exclaimed impatiently. "Have I got to live to the end of my days without reading anything, and wearing skirts two feet too long! I hate them!"

"Yes, and so do I," agreed Gram. "But, dearest, we must be getting back. All the men-folks have gone up to Fort Sumner to try and sell their cattle, and the women are down in that tent, singing. This opportunity may never happen again; but where are *you* going, Mr. McCutcheon?"

"Never mind," he said. "Away from here — I'll never see you again. But where are you going? To California?"

"Nobody knows. It may be to Arizona or we may settle down in this lovely place. But conditions became so desperate back on the Brazos that we just got up and *moved*. But I want to know you — sometime," quavered Musette. "My father and mother don't approve of my ways and very soon I shall be a woman. Then they will compel me to marry some man; but, Beau, I want to know *you*. I know you broke jail at Fort Davis; Mother says you consort with bad men. But I know you are good and, when the time comes I'd rather marry you. That is, if you still want me."

"I do," he said, glancing across at Gram as he gave her a friendly kiss. "You're all I think about while I lie here waiting and I'm sorry your mother doesn't like me —"

59

"And all I think of is you," declared Musette. "I don't care what she says. But I couldn't rest or sleep, for fear you would go away and I'd never get to say what I think. But ever since you saved me I feel that I belong to you. Only, of course —"

"We'll have to wait," he nodded. "But I had been reading one of the greatest love stories ever written, and Juliet was only fourteen."

"Oh, *was* she?" she laughed back triumphantly. "I'm going on fifteen, myself. But Gram has always been my friend. She told me it would be all right if I came over to see you, although my mother is very strict. And Ash, he always watches me —"

She fell silent, for the meeting had broken up and Gram had risen to her feet.

"She was afraid you would go without her ever seeing you," the old lady explained. "And — well, Mr. McCutcheon, good-by."

She climbed nimbly on her horse and Beau saw the reason why. Elvina Haught had looked across and seen them and was coming on the run. But Musette was looking up at him with tears in her eyes, and she did not shrink away.

"Aren't you going to help me — up on my horse?" she asked, and McCutcheon leaned down to lift her.

"Of course I am," he said and kissed her again, before he swung her up.

"Here! What are you doing?" demanded Mrs. Haught, shrilly. "I declare, if it isn't that Beau! Now you leave that child alone, Mr. McCutcheon," she stormed, "or I won't be accountable for what I do!"

60

"You never are," he answered back, defiantly, "and I might as well tell you that Musette and I are going to get married. We've talked it all over and —"

"Oh, here's your book," he ended, passing Musette her *Romeo and Juliet* as her mother snatched her away. And Musette held it close.

CHAPTER
NINE

Protracted Meetings

That there was no love lost between McCutcheon and Elvina Haught anyone could see at a glance. He stood right up to her when she started to scold him, and she took it out on the girl.

"You Musette," she began, "what are you doing over here in the camp of this strange man? You ought to be in the wagon, recovering from your accident, and here you are, with *him*!"

"She couldn't sleep or rest," answered Gram, "until she thanked him for saving her life. So I took her over, while you were going to the meeting — and Mr. McCutcheon is a perfect gentleman. He got his head hurt in a battle with the Indians, and he's been here ever since. He's a son of Jim McCutcheon, of Waxahatchie, Texas, and —"

"Didn't he break out of jail? Didn't he steal that Ranger's horse? Well, Gram, I'm surprised at you, and I'm going to forbid you to have anything more to do with my children —"

"You *cain't* forbid me," came back Gram. "Henry Haught is my son — as good a man as ever lived — and if he saw how you are running around with that preacher —"

"Now you shut up!" challenged Elvina, and Gram winked at Beau as she laughed.

"You take care of your morals and I'll take care of mine," she advised. "There's very few, if any, of us that haven't made a few mistakes, but Musette is my favorite grandchild and I won't stand to see her abused."

She put her arm around Musette, rode back to the wagons and Beau turned back and lay down. He was thoroughly disgusted with the actions of Mrs. Haught — and equally disgusted with the evangelist. Just that afternoon he had driven in down the north trail, which was taking so many people to California, and hardly had his strikers put up the well-worn tent when the whole Haught family swarmed into it. The preacher was a man of experience, having seen women like her before, and after telling five stories about hunting coons in Arkansaw he knelt down and began to pray. Then he sang — good old songs about love and salvation — and when he got around to his exhortation, half the crowd was at the mourners' bench.

It might be religion, but Beau did not like it, and they were going to continue that night. For three days and nights the band of Haught women had been suffering for some emotional outlet, and this old preacher with his broad shoulders and bearded jowls offered just the relief they wanted. Nor were the women the only ones to get his message. Martin Hockaday had gone down before the first tent was up and invited the whole company to supper and when the Haught outfit returned from Fort Sumner they found Hockaday and half his cowboys singing and patting their hands.

Red Ryan sat beside the fair Odette, who was inquiring about his soul's salvation, and Red had a series of confessions to recite that drove Gram out of the tent. She had a hunch that Ryan was possessed of some ulterior motive not associated with religion and the Haught men were very glum. After a long ride to the Fort they had found the contracts all let and it would be necessary to go clear to Santa Fe to make a bid on the next one. Moreover, a man named Adams had so underbid the rest as to give credence to the report that he was venal — that he had no intention of meeting his contracts, but was merely trying to break the market. And the rumor was afloat that all Texans would be barred for alleged disloyalty to the Government.

This was a last blow to their hopes for a ready sale and they were talking about going on; but when Hockaday heard them ride in he hurried out to meet them and brought them into the tent. It was a general rule of this Cattle King, who ruled the Pecos for two hundred miles, that no trail herd could enter or leave his domain without being cut — twice. Once when they entered Deep Lake, after picking up the mavericks on his range; and once more when they left his range, with more or less strays in their possession. And yet, when Hockaday's warriors cut them down to their trail brand, almost all the Texans objected.

Some objected violently, and that was what the warriors were for. Martin Hockaday had a hundred and fifty powers of attorney, authorizing him to seize Texas cattle found in New Mexico but not in the present owner's brands, and sell them for one half the profits. Most of these cattle had been stolen by the Comanches and sold to the Mexican ranchers. Others had been picked up from the open range in Western Texas when the trail-masters were going through. It was the general practice, when driving to Arizona, to drift all the stray cattle into the main herd, and no questions were asked.

But Martin Hockaday, though he made everybody welcome and had never charged for a meal in his life, had to strip the passing herds clean or he wouldn't have a beef steer left. The Texans had been very careless — they admitted it themselves — but at the same time they objected to the cut. And, until his two nephews got in with their herd, Hockaday was sitting tight. So, if he could keep the Haught family contented, with good water, free grass and free meals, it would be better, all around. After Captain Jack had accepted the herd which John and Lester had gone to get — the market would probably ease off a little, although other herds were moving north.

In an era of big movements, of trouble and of strife, Martin was always for peace. He never carried a pistol — except on the few occasions when it was absolutely necessary to use it — and for every cow that he stole he lost ten to the rustlers who had gathered on the edge of his range. He was honest, as cowmen go, but at times he had to be firm. And Hightower would soon be back.

His was the one herd that was never questioned or cut. He bought nothing but longhorn steers, from the bottomlands of the Brazos. He branded every one of them in the chutes before he started out and, out of courtesy, he cut his whole herd again before he left Deep Lake.

That was why he never forgave Henry Haught for daring to question his count. And when he heard about the eighteen neighbors found hung by the neck with horse-hobbles, he and his men were ready to fight. But Captain Jack had something to do besides mix in on a family feud, and he had always found Hockaday honest. They had ridden the trail together until Martin had settled down, brought in she-stuff and begun to build up a herd. Now Hightower was paying him a dollar a head extra for every steer he accepted and picking them up as he passed.

There was a tremendous rush of cattle into Colorado, where the mines were opening up; and with a quiet bunch of men, well-versed in the trailing business, he was making money hand over fist. When the other drovers from Texas underbid him on his Indian contracts he pushed right on into Denver, making a new trail as he went. Some called him The Trail-maker; but he was a law-maker, too. And the stealing was getting very bad. There were men on the Brazos who made a business of branding mavericks, but they never sold to him.

The last time he passed Deep Lake he had not even stopped to eat. Henry Haught, who had insulted him, had dared to offer to sell him more cattle — after demanding a cut on his herd. But with the easygoing Hockaday it was different — and Martin was strong for religion. He loved to sing and pray, pat his hands and confess his sins; and with all the Haught women to talk with he let the world go by. He loved the sound of women's voices, the deep emotion of their appeals, the sight of their fair faces, covered with tears; and if his warriors quit work to join in on the protracted meeting, it was all the same to him. Only — when the Haughts left — it was their duty to cut the herds, now reduced to eight thousand head.

He put off the evil day when he had to inform them that a quarter of their cows must be left. The law applied equally to Mexicans and Texans, to men under arms and Indians with war-bonnets. He had, wrapped up in a section of zinc pipe, powers of attorney to claim half the brands in western Texas, though he never felt it necessary to show them. And if, after cutting out the strays, he never felt called upon to sell them and give the distant owners half the profits, the rustlers in the mountains to the west were doing the same with him.

For ten days his life had been like a dream, full of hope and the sweet expectation of winning salvation and love; and then, when his nephews brought in their second herd, he realized that something was wrong. The brands were not right and, although they had whipped off the bloodthirsty Comanches, he knew that Jack Hightower would never accept these steers. The boys had stolen the first cattle they had come upon, just as their uncle had ordered them, and now it was too late to change.

But one thing he could do — he could cut every maverick out of Henry Haught's herd and give them all a hair brand. It was quick, it was sure, and he had time to do it; but the Haught women would never smile on him again.

CHAPTER
TEN

The Last Night

The Haught men-folks had been clamoring for days to hit the trail and go, but Elvina had been fascinated by the songs and sermons of the preacher, his stories about hunting coons in the swamps while he was "water-bound in Arkansaw." Now they rebelled against the tyranny of their women and the next morning they decided to start. After all, it was Henry Haught that did their thinking for them; and, right or wrong, they did what he said.

Their cattle had been held, loose-herded, ever since they had stopped at Deep Lake, but when they drove them down for a last drink of sweet water, Martin Hockaday and his warriors rode out. Everybody knew that he always cut the cattle, and yet they could hardly believe it. He had always been so friendly, so hospitable and kind, and he had only seven warriors.

"Going out?" he inquired; and when Haught nodded, Martin turned and spoke to his men.

"Cut 'em down to their trail-brand," he directed; and that meant a thousand head.

"By what authority?" demanded Henry Haught; and Hockaday opened up his powers of attorney, the first time he had ever shown them. He had collected them in western Texas when the cows had no value, except for the hides and tallow.

"The State of Texas," he answered. "These owners have authorized me to seize every cow-brute that I find in New Mexico and sell it for half the profits. Sorry to see you go, but that's my ironclad contract."

"It may be all that," retorted Haught, "and yet not work in this case. I have kept my cattle loose-herded every minute, there isn't a maverick in the bunch; and I'm here to inform you, Mr. Hockaday, that you can't cut a single cow."

"These are my warriors." said Hockaday, waving his hand towards Red Ryan and his men, "and their orders are to cut your herd. Are you going to do it, boys? Eh, Red?"

"Sure as hell," returned Ryan. "You don't look bad to me, Mr. Haught. Never did and never will. Any time you're ready you can just start shooting, and I'll bet I beat you to it."

He shifted his pistol a little nearer to the front and Henry Haught beckoned up his men.

"Well, boys," he said. "What are you going to do about it? Look those papers over first," he suggested to his brother Si. "And one thing I'll say right now. If we can't go north we can keep on going west until we end up in Arizona."

"The papers are all right," reported Haught at last. "How about it, Mr. Hockaday? Suppose we stay right here. What then?"

"Stay as long as you want to," answered Hockaday politely. "But you don't go any further north until we cut your herd."

"We'll stay, then," decided Henry Haught promptly. "I was looking for something like this, Mr. Hockaday. You've been too good to be true. But as long as there's a road to the west we'll just keep on to Arizona."

"You bet ye!" chorused his cowboys and turned their cattle out on the plain.

It extended forty miles east and west, and two hundred miles, north and south, watered all the way by the Pecos River, with grass a foot deep everywhere. Not even in Texas was there a range so magnificent, and yet it was held by one man. A little, insignificant man who hardly ever wore a six-shooter. The Apaches could have killed him long ago, but they decided to let him live, for, with him gone, who else was there to bring in so many horses and cattle?

The Haughts could have killed him, too, if they had had the nerve, but they decided to let him live. It was open range in every direction, he had said that he needed neighbors; and, with all the women folks to entertain him and listen to his experiences, they were safe for one more night. Their protracted meetings had reached a height of glory where they wanted to sign and dance; but, just in case something might happen, Haught posted a double guard. Then, after dark, he called out every man, for they had had two or three stampedes.

Let the women get the glory if they wanted to. Henry Haught had been bred on the Texas frontier, where anything was likely to happen. They might have a big stampede, with all their cattle scattered and mixed up with Hockaday's cows. Then they would have a cut — maybe started by the Indians, maybe started by somebody else. It was two days after the full moon, when the Comanches made their raids, and Haught didn't put it past this psalm-singing Cattle King to start the stampede himself.

Personally, Henry Haught distrusted all preachers, especially since Elvina had got religion at a camp meeting and had been on the edge ever since. He hated evangelists on general principles, but he let her attend the meetings. It would keep Martin Hockaday out of mischief — and all seven of his warriors were there. A little rough, perhaps, in the way they danced with the ladies; but then, the whole country was rough. These particular warriors had broken jail at Fort Davis and every one of them was on the dodge. Beau McCutcheon, their former leader, was hiding out from the Rangers and keeping carefully out of sight.

Not since little Musette had ridden over with her grandmother and pledged him her heart and hand, had McCutcheon seen his loved one, yet he still watched the wagons where her folks were camped, and still hoped that his dreams were true. He had hoped she still would come — before they went away — and give him another kiss. Thank him again for saving her life and pledge it all to him. He was young — he had nothing and was on the dodge — but youth must have its dreams.

She came, just after sundown, when the singing began and the kerosene torches flared up in the tent, where all the people had gone in. She was dressed in her best — the same velvet riding-habit she had worn on that fatal day. And for convenience when she walked — with two feet of trailing skirt — she caught it up with a silver chatelaine. Her face was concealed beneath a heavy veil, the russet gown looked black in the dark. She stood up, straight and slender, though a little small. But then, she was only fourteen.

With a little girl like her he did not feel bashful; and when she appeared in the twilight, he hurried out to meet her.

"I just came out to see you," she said. "Even Gram doesn't know I'm gone. But — I had to return your book."

She thrust it into his hand and started to go, and Beau did not call her back. But the voice of her mother, singing psalms in the tent, encouraged her to stop and hurry back.

"You don't know," she said, "how many times I've read it, while I was lying there in the wagon. Did it really happen? Could it possibly be true? Was there ever a girl like that?"

"I like to think so," he answered, giving it back to her. "And I want you to keep it — always. Yes, there was a Juliet, of the house of Capulet, and she loved Romeo until she died."

"And did men fight like that — for nothing, almost? Why, Beau, it was almost like *now!* All the Haughts are like that — they're trying to make me marry and I'm

73

only fourteen. Like her. And that scene in the garden, when he climbed up to her window and spoke such beautiful words! Oh, tell me, could that be true? I wanted to see you and find out about it before we all went away. But Gram wouldn't let me — until tonight. Then she dressed me up in my elegant new riding suit and told me I might go. Are you ever going to see me again," she said, "or is it all a dream? Let's sit over here — out of sight."

She drew him into the shadow of a cottonwood — and as she walked he noticed that she limped — but when she sat down on the bank above the ditch, she reached over and touched his head.

"Are you getting well?" she asked. "Does that wound still bother you? Oh, you seem like a knight, fighting battles, but my mother says you're an *outlaw*. She says you're hiding out for fear the Rangers will catch you. She says you stole a horse."

"Yes, I did," admitted Beau. "And the horse was a good one, too. But Captain Hightower gave me another one, for whipping off these Comanches, and he's going to give the first one back to the Ranger. It's a man he knows — Rye Miles —"

"And aren't you hiding out," she cried, "at all? Oh, Beau!" And she kissed him. "Then we can get married — sometime. Can't we?"

"Well, that's what I hoped," he said. "Does your grandmother think I'm all right?"

"She just loves you! She thinks you're wonderful! But she says we're both too young."

"We are! We are!" he answered. "But don't let them marry you off. And when you grow up, I'll have a ranch and everything. Captain Hightower is going to give me a job. When he found I wouldn't work for Hockaday because he wanted me to cut the herds he said I was just the man he was looking for. 'An honest man,' he said. 'An honest man.' He says he's got a job that calls for a little nerve, but he saw me when I fought off those Comanches; and if it hadn't been for me and the rest of the boys they'd have stolen every horse he had."

"But this Red Ryan! You don't like him, do you? He's making love to Odette, but Gram says he is crooked. He's a bad one! He's on the dodge!"

"So am I," he laughed. "But Captain Hightower will square me. He knows this Rye Miles and when he sent the horse back he told him I was a very good man. A man of principle. One he could trust."

"I'm going right back and tell that to Grandma," declared Musette, jumping up. But she tripped in her long skirt and sat down — hard; and Beau had to pick her up again.

"You're gaining weight," he said, moving closer beside her. "It won't be long until you're big enough to marry me. But when can I see you again?"

"I don't know," she sighed. "My mother doesn't like you and — Oh, the meeting is breaking up! Or is it just somebody coming?"

She paused as a young couple came hurrying up the path, and gasped as she moved away from Beau. It was Odette, tall and handsome; and beside her, holding her

75

hand, ran Ryan. They went by without seeing them, but near the house she stopped short.

"Where are you taking me to, Red Ryan?" she asked; and he tried to steal a kiss.

"You know!" he laughed and she slapped him over backwards.

"I hate you," she cried, running away; and when she passed them she was sobbing.

"I think I'd better go," said Musette in a still, small voice; and McCutcheon let her pass.

It was so unusual, so unexpected, Odette slipping off this way with Red; the quarrel and her coming back. Not the usual lovers' quarrel. It had a sinister note. For Ryan came rushing down the pathway, spitting out vulgar oaths as he passed.

But Musette returned and stood close to Beau and he heard her breathing hard.

"You're not like that, are you, Beau?" she asked; and stood a long time, listening.

"As soon as the meeting breaks up," she began. Then a form in the distance moved towards them.

It was Ash, tall and menacing, a pistol on his hip, and without a word he hit Beau on the jaw.

"Go on back to your mother," he commanded Musette, and turned back to strike Beau again.

"So this is what you're up to," he cursed, "you and that so-and-so, Red."

"What?" cried McCutcheon, striking out at him; and Ash Haught went down like a log.

He was a big man and a violent one, taking advantage of his weight; but when he scrambled up

Beau knocked him down again. Then he snatched him up, still raging, and smashed him over the head with his pistol barrel.

They were still fighting away, half groggy from their beating but blind with hatred and pain, when the earth itself seemed to tremble beneath their feet. There was a roar like distant thunder, the pounding of thousands of feet, and in an instant the herd was off.

"God!" cried Ash. "A stampede!"

He flung down his opponent and was gone.

CHAPTER
ELEVEN

The Stampede

Nobody knew what had started the cattle. One moment they were lying down, close-guarded by armed men; the next instant they were off with a savage clacking of hoofs, the clashing of thousands of horns. As their heads struck together there was a flash like sheet lightning, the horses ran like the wind and the great stampede was on.

Men rode on the left side, turning the herd to the right, trying to mill them and tie them up in a knot; but something had stampeded every cow in the herd, they sensed some invisible presence and were gone. They outran the fleetest horses across the open plains and at daylight they were miles away. Then, wearily, they turned back, still afraid of that Something that human eye could never see. Only now they were mixed in the wildest confusion. And there would have to be a cut.

Greater than the terror of a lightning blast, striking in the middle of the herd, was this panic which nobody could understand but which left every cowbrute wild. They came back in scattered bunches, cows separated from their calves, steers still running as they remembered their fright, and no one could accuse the warriors of Martin Hockaday, because every man had been at the meeting. Hockaday had been there, and Ash Haught had been fighting Beau McCutcheon.

At the moment they had been locked in a blind, senseless combat, which neither of them tried to explain. At a word, a mere implication, they had closed in sudden battle. Ash's head was bloody, Beau's head was bruised and red; and as long as they lived they would burn with unreasoning hate. And before they could cut every maverick in the herd — every Lightning Rod, every Long Rail, every Jingle-bob — the Haughts had lost another thousand head of cattle and were mad enough to fight. Red Ryan was up in front with his pistol in his hand, and he trimmed them down to their trail-brand. At a mere word from Ash Haught he had struck him off his horse. His gun was gory with hair and blood, and he invited the whole clan to draw and shoot. Then, at the end, he called Odette a name which no gentleman would use.

And yet Ash was afraid to take him up on it, for Ryan was just waiting to shoot. The preacher moved his tent without waiting to pull up the stakes and Hockaday did not ask him to stay. There was blood on the moon when Jack Hightower rode in and asked for his thousand head of cows. He had signed a contract with the sutler at Fort Sumner to deliver that many cattle. Not that Jack wanted them, or would make any profit — for Andy Adams had knocked the price to almost nothing — but he had given his word to deliver this mixed lot and one look at Hockaday's cows was enough.

"There's some mistake here," he said to his old-time partner. "Every one of these cows has been hair-branded. Where's your bills of sale?"

"I haven't got any," replied Martin humbly. "These boys lost their first herd to the Comanche Indians and I told them to go back and get more. Grab the first thousand cows they could ketch on the open range and get them here on time. So here they are. The Indians won't know the difference and —"

"Do you expect me to accept these cattle?" demanded Hightower, "when you know every cow has been stolen? Well, things have gone to hell in the Pecos River country when Martin Hockaday turns crook, and I'll have to put my foot *down*. I'll have to take a loss under my contract, but I refuse to accept these cows."

"Then here's my own herd," protested Hockaday. "I'll take the loss myself. Or here's this bunch of cows that I've just cut from Haught's herd. You can take your pick from that."

"I'll never accept a cow that Henry Haught ever owned," answered Captain Hightower, angrily. "He done doubted my word by demanding that cut and both of you can go to hell. What this country needs is a little plain honesty. And by the way, where's Beau McCutcheon?"

"He's around here somewhere," answered Hockaday sullenly. "And Mr. Haught, you can move your cattle. Move 'em north or move 'em west, it's no difference to me now; but git 'em off my range."

"Yes, you old tarrapin," cursed back Haught. "You've got your cut, so I can go, eh? I'd jest like to know what caused that stompede and mixed our herds all up. I would so."

"Well, so would I," yelled back Hockaday. "But you can't say it was me, or any of my men. Every one of us was here, attending divine service, so take your cattle, and go."

"Turn 'em west, boys," shouted Haught, waving his hat as a signal. "And, Mr. Hockaday, we'll meet again."

"Any time, sir. Any time!" answered Martin, as his enemy rode off; and Captain Hightower regarded him reprovingly.

"I wish I had ten Texas Rangers here," he said, "and I'd make you both hunt your holes. But go your way, Martin Hockaday, and I'll go mine. I'll never buy from you again."

He rode off, still rumbling, and when he saw Beau McCutcheon, lying under his tree, he threw up his hands in despair.

"Fighting, eh?" he grunted. "Head all beat up again. Well, I sent that horse back to Rye Miles at Fort Davis and I haven't heard a word out of him since."

"Never mind," said Beau. "I'm going west, anyway, and it really doesn't make any difference."

"It makes this difference," came back Hightower. "You've returned a horse you stole and, as far as I know, your conscience is clear. You can ride the trail now without looking over your shoulder for some Texas Ranger to show up. I was beginning to like you, young man, and I was going to offer you a job."

"Keep it," returned McCutcheon, without getting up. "I'm a miserable failure, and no good to you anyhow —"

"Who hit you over the head?" inquired Captain Jack.

"Ash Haught," answered Beau.

"I hear the Haughts are going west," suggested Hightower. And McCutcheon sat up with a jerk. Then he sank down wearily and felt his sore head, which was wrapped up in another white rag.

"Mr. McCutcheon," went on Captain Jack. "I don't ordinarily presume to give a young man any advice but in this case I'll make an exception. I can use you, sore head and all, for a hundred dollars a month. For a little detective work. I stand, in a few years, to make hundreds of thousands of dollars in my business as a trail-boss; but if this fighting keeps on I'm liable to lose everything, and maybe get killed, to boot. Here my old friend, Martin Hockaday, that I began riding the trail with, has gone back to his old ways of stealing cows. Last year he hired some men, a bunch of buffalo hunters, to cut these herds when they passed; but they quit him to work for another man, stealing cattle at five dollars a head.

"Now he's took on Red Ryan and his friends and they've just trimmed this Henry Haught. But it won't be long till they begin to figure out that working for the boss doesn't pay. Then *they'll* quit and begin stealing for themselves. Turn around, probably, and steal from him. The next thing you know there'll be a range war on and a lot of good men will get killed."

"Even so," said Beau. "Where do I come in?"

"You and your sore head, wrapped up in a white rag, are worth a hundred a month to me. The Indians will all know you — cowboys and Mexicans too — and I just want you to ride around. Pick up all the information you can and report to me every month. Your personal affairs are nothing to me, but if you can follow this Haught outfit and find out what they're up to, it will be satisfactory to me. I heard over on the Brazos that they hung eighteen men when they left; but every one of those men was a cattle-thief, so that wipes the slate clean, for me. If there's any man in the world I hate and despise —"

"I'll take the job," answered Beau.

CHAPTER
TWELVE

Lincoln

The road to California led off to the west, heading for blue mountains, far away — the timbered heights of the Sierra Blancas. It passed through the Reservation of the Mescalero Apaches, who had only recently been on the warpath, but the soldiers at Fort Stanton now had them under control, while the Government fed them beef to keep them quiet.

There was rich feed from Deep Lake to the wide canyon of the Hondo, where the river disappeared, coming out on the plains below. Or that was what everybody thought. All they knew was that the stream furnished water for man and beast, until it went underground.

But the herds of Henry Haught, after the stampede of the night before, barely moved up the overland trail, and Beau McCutcheon went past them without being seen, taking the first road to the right at Hondo. To the left another road turned up the broad valley of the Ruidoso, leading over the mountains to the west. But Lincoln, up the Bonito, was the town that caught all the trade for a hundred miles each way. A new town, built up by the presence of Fort Stanton, and living chiefly by its stores and saloons.

Beau's mustang, re-named Hot Foot, took the road on a jog trot that landed them in town the same day; and as he passed up the street every eye was upon him. He felt that he was being watched. Then a tall man with that officer-look about him rose up from his seat on a stone wall and brought him to a halt.

"Where did you get that horse, young man?" he asked and flashed his deputy's star.

"From Captain Jack Hightower, if it's any of your business," answered Beau, and the deputy looked him over again.

"What's the matter with your head?" he inquired suspiciously. "Seems to me I've seen you before."

"Not here," returned McCutcheon, and kept on to the big corral. But as he was feeding his horse the deputy followed him, with an interest that would not be downed.

"Looking for a job?" he asked, and Beau shook his head.

"Just passing through," he said.

"Better stay," advised the deputy. "It's a live town, and no mistake. There's a fellow down below here that's got a beef contract. Name's Butch Hardigan and — tell him I sent you. But Major O'Grady owns half the town — the store, the hotel and everything. Did you come up from Deep Lake today?"

"Yes," shrugged Beau. "Were you looking for somebody? Perhaps you were looking for *me*?"

"Not at all, Mr. McCutcheon," answered the deputy sheriff, cordially. "How's the Captain getting along? Hear you had a big stampede over at Deep Lake last night? Was you in on it, by any chance?"

"No," answered Beau. "I was not. Now let me ask you one. Have you got any papers for me?"

"Nary a paper," replied the deputy, grinning. "Jest saw you were a stranger in town."

"Well, in that case," said Beau, "you can pull that auger out while I get a little something to eat."

He hurried over to the lunch counter but he had hardly sat down when another officer sat down beside him. A tall man, and his badge said "Sheriff."

"About that horse," he began. "Are you sure it didn't come from Fort Davis? We've had a letter from Rye Miles of the Texas Rangers — to look out for a bay horse with a black mane and tail —"

"This horse is branded HT on the left hip," broke in McCutcheon. "Are you looking for a horse with that iron? Well, leave me alone then and let me eat this beefsteak. I came off without my breakfast."

This was no way to talk to a sheriff — with his deputy just outside the door — but after thinking it over the officer rose up in stony silence and ordered a steak for himself. For a small town, with one store and two saloons and half the population Mexicans, it seemed to Beau to be badly overstaffed with officers. But there was something going on for, before he had finished, another important man walked in.

He was a gentleman of military appearance, long mustaches and a commanding eye. A man of parts,

Beau could see that at a glance, but his approach was different from the rest.

"Good evening, sir," he greeted. "I am Major O'Grady, the proprietor of this hotel. I hope you find the service satisfactory. I wonder if you could tell me about this herd, belonging to Colonel Haught, which is coming up the road?"

He smiled so affably that McCutcheon was won over from the start.

"Glad to do so," he said. "Although I don't know the gentleman. He had a big stampede last night, lost over a thousand cows and is heading for Arizona."

"So I hear, so I hear," murmured O'Grady, doubtfully. "You don't happen to know whether he's thinking of settling down here? I am the owner of a large ranch down at Seven Rivers — a neighbor, you might say, of Martin Hockaday — and, naturally, I take a personal interest. Because if these Texas cowmen ever settle in these parts there'll be more trouble than would pack hell a mile — if you'll excuse the expression, Mister McCutcheon. I'd rather have Hockaday as a friend than a neighbor. He cuts every herd that goes through Deep Lake, keeping open house to the cowmen all the time; and for a dollar's worth of beans he'll take a thousand dollars' worth of cattle and send you on your way with a smile. I hope old Martin isn't a personal friend of yours, because —"

"He is," spoke up Beau. "I've been camping at Deep Lake for two weeks and the old man has treated me fine. Sent a boy out every morning with a cup of coffee —"

"That's it!" exclaimed O'Grady, bitterly. "But take this Haught outfit, now. He invited them right in, never charged them a cent, went to camp meeting with the women and everything. And the day they start to go he sends out his warriors and steals a thousand head of their cattle. Or fifteen hundred would be more like it, because he started a big stampede in the middle of the night and scattered them for forty miles. There's five hundred head left on his range that never will be took, except by rustlers; and what authority did he ever have for trimming their herd in the first place?"

"He showed Henry Haught his powers of attorney for a hundred and fifty brands —"

"*Showed* 'em to him!" demanded the Major; and while they were arguing the matter there was a clatter of hoofs outside. Fifteen or twenty cowboys dropped off their horses and headed for the bar, and O'Grady beckoned to one of them.

"Come over here, Jesse," he commanded, as their leader ordered the drinks. "You've worked for Martin Hockaday — how did he treat you?"

Jesse Mowbray was attired in the height of cowboy fashion — wearing velveteen trousers and two pearl-handled six-shooters. But he waited for his drink before he made reply, glancing curiously at McCutcheon the while.

"Oh, fine!" he responded, looking back at the boys, and they joined in a general laugh. "Fine as silk," went on Mowbray. "The drinks were always free, the grub was good, bunch of Mexicans to do all the work. Only what was the use of stealing all those cattle for *him* when we might steal 'em for ourselves?"

"I'll introduce you," began the Major sternly, "to Beau McCutcheon, just up from Deep Lake. He says that Martin Hockaday has the powers of attorney for a hundred and fifty Texas brands. Ever hear of anything like that?"

"Well — yes," replied Mowbray, while the cowboys gathered around. "But we never *seen* any! Eh, boys?"

"Not any," answered big Bill Nuckels. "All we had to do was cut the strays. But Martin always said he had 'em."

"Well, he's got 'em!" stated O'Grady. "He showed 'em to Henry Haught, and Haught let them cut his herd. Now Haught is coming west over the trail, and the question is — what are we going to do about it?"

"You tell 'em!" grinned Mowbray. "What's the answer?"

"Push our stuff out of the way. Let 'em pass, but don't encourage 'em to stop. That's all, boys — have a drink on me."

The cowboys trooped back to the bar, Beau returned to his beefsteak and O'Grady sat in gloomy silence.

"Are you friends with the Haughts?" he asked at last; and McCutcheon shrugged, saying nothing.

"I don't want to pry into your personal affairs," said O'Grady. "But I take it for granted you're against them."

"It makes no difference," answered Beau, "I'm hitting the trail in the morning. Unless, of course, your sheriff and deputy want to ask some more questions about that *horse*."

"Certainly not," replied O'Grady. "I'm sorry they troubled you. Only it is rather unusual to have a man coming through that's rode off on a Ranger's horse."

"This horse —" began McCutcheon; and then he stopped. He was going to say that Hot Foot did not belong to the Ranger, that he was a present to him from Captain Hightower as a reward for standing off the Comanches; but if the boss of Lincoln preferred to consider him a thief it was all right with cattle detective McCutcheon.

"John," spoke up O'Grady, jerking his head at the sullen sheriff, "report to Mr. Miles that the horse did not come through here, but we will keep a close lookout for strangers. It isn't the first time a Texas Ranger has been put afoot. But this ain't Texas, is it?"

"No," answered Beau, and laughed.

"As a matter of fact," smiled O'Grady, "some of our best and most useful citizens have stepped across the line; and as long as you will answer a few questions it will be all right with me. And, now that I'm on the subject, I elected Sheriff Haley, personally. It is always convenient for me, however, to have a few friends on the outside, and I am especially interested at the moment in hearing about Henry Haught. Is it a fact, do you know, that he hung eighteen men with horse-hobbles when they followed him away from the Brazos? That is a sign of a certain determination of character. Would you advise me to make friends with this man? I might as well tell you I am fighting Martin Hockaday with every weapon at my command."

"You'd better let Mr. Haught alone," observed Beau, and O'Grady nodded gravely.

"At the same time," he went on, "there's no escaping the fact that he let Red Ryan cut his herd. Now, what do you think of Ryan?"

"He's dangerous," shrugged McCutcheon, despondently. "Stood up to Ash Haught and smashed him over the head with his six-shooter; and if Ash had made a play he'd have killed him."

"Ah-h!" nodded O'Grady, "that explains things. Red is the man I'm looking for. Well, that's all, Mr. McCutcheon, and I'm proud to shake hands with a man that had the nerve to rob a Ranger. At the same time I'd advise you to keep on going, as Rye Miles is on the prod. He has the name of being a vindictive cuss, and I reckon you know about the Rangers. When they reach the State line they just take off their badges and keep going, as private citizens."

CHAPTER
THIRTEEN

The Sheriff of Doña Ana

There was an element of truth in O'Grady's remarks about the Texas Rangers. They never let the Line stand in their way — just took off their badge, if they happened to have one, and kept going as private individuals. Beau McCutcheon remembered this when he woke up at daylight and, without stopping for the ham and eggs, he rode out the main street, west. It disappeared in a clump of maples and oaks and came out above a Mexican ranch. He tied Hot Foot in front of the house and had gone in to have a dish of beans, when a huge shadow fell across the doorway.

"Whose harse is that?" inquired a broad Irish voice, and McCutcheon drew his gun.

"Mine!" he answered, looking around the corner; and his visitor burst out laughing.

"No harm," he said. "No harm at all. I was jist going by when I saw this fine harse, in front of the house of my old friend, Ygenio Salazar, and I says to myself: 'There's that bay harse with a black mane and tail that the boys have been looking for everywhere.' But I

wasn't expecting to find you here at all, Misther — ah
— Misther —"

"McCutcheon!" answered Beau.

"Ah, how do you do, Misther McCutcheon!" hailed
the stranger. "I'm Butch Hardigan, the fort butcher at
Fort Stanton."

"There's something queer about this horse,"
observed Beau impatiently. "Do you notice that HT on
its hip? I've got a bill of sale in my pocket —"

"To be sure. To be sure!" exclaimed Hardigan, "but
who made out this bill of sale? Not that it matters, of
carse, but you've got your thumb over the signature."

"Yes, and I'm going to keep it there," stated
McCutcheon, "until you go on away and mind your
own business. Now who is this man that's lost a bay
horse, with a black mane and tail?"

"Why, Rye Miles, of carse. He's searching for it
everywhere."

"Anything said about a brand on its left hip, HT?
I've been told by men who ought to know that that's
the commonest color for old-time mustangs — bay,
with a black mane and tail. So if Mrs. Salazar will
kindly give me some more beans —"

"Oh, excuse me! A thousand pardons!" cried
Hardigan. "When I get into Lincoln I'll be sure to tell
the byes it's another harse, branded HT."

"Please do so," grumbled Beau, turning back to his
breakfast; and Butch Hardigan began his line of talk.

"Are you going right through Lincoln, Misther
McCutcheon," he asked, "without stopping to see the
town at all? I observe by your boots you're a cowboy,

yourself, and you're passing up something very good. Of all the countries I ever stopped in, this has got them all beat for mavericks. Thousands and thousands of them, three and four years old, the property of the first man that brands them.

"As butcher for the soldiers at Fort Stanton I pay five dollars a head for steers — maverick steers, you understand — without a brand or earmark on them. 'Tis a perfectly legitimate business, overseen at every point by the Government. All you have to do is bring in a bunch of mavericks — or others with a brand that don't show — and I'll pay you cash on the nail."

"No, I'm sorry," said Beau, rising up and laying a quarter on the table, "but I can't stop, even for five dollars. Many thanks, Mrs. Salazar, for your frijoles —"

"What? Are you going away?" exclaimed Butch Hardigan; and, behind his back, Ygenio nodded warningly.

"I am," returned McCutcheon, "unless you've got some violent objections. Good-by, Mr. Salazar, and thanks for your kind hospitality."

He had mounted to go, carefully facing Butch as he did so, when Hardigan made a last try. That he planned some evil was obvious by his horse-face alone. His bulging black eyes, heavy jaw and hairy hands seemed designed by Nature to warn people.

"There's a short trail over the mountains," he said, "that will save you twenty miles at the least, if you're going to Las Cruces." And once more, behind his back, the friendly Mexican shook his head.

"I'm not going to Las Cruces," Beau answered, and rode off up the trail.

Mr. Hardigan had a businesslike-looking pistol, hanging low on his hip in a rawhide holster, which he seemed very anxious not to show; yet, as well as he knew anything, Beau knew it would come out the moment he turned his back. There must be a reward up for a man of his general description and his greatest safety lay in flight.

The trail led on to the north and the west, in the shadow of mighty Capitan and he kept Hot Foot on the jump until they swung up over the divide. Then he turned off on a dim trail and hid out for the day, descending to the White Sands after dark. It was a valley so wide and dry that hardly a trail led across it; yet, athwart its middle, lay a gigantic lava bed, half buried in the sands. Beau watered his horse at a well by the wayside, against the slope of the sand hills, and the next morning at dawn he saw, to the east, the dust of Henry Haught's herd.

They were driving them hard, down the winding Ruidoso, where the river led out onto the plain; and, far away on the desert of white gypsum sand, Beau followed them to the west. In the distance McCutcheon could see the black-trousered cowboys pushing their scattered cattle out of the way, carrying out O'Grady's orders to clear the way for these fighting invaders from Texas.

In the northern end of the valley there was water, and feed and shelter, but the road led the other way to

Las Cruces on the Rio Grande — and thence to Arizona.

"Do not encourage them to stop," had been O'Grady's last command and the cowboys were keeping the road open. The fact that the stage had stopped running, that all travel over the Overland Trail had ceased, made no difference to the Haughts, as they passed through the Apache Reservation. The tracks of many cattle led on ahead of them, but Jesse Mowbray and his men avoided them. The seven or eight thousand cattle were like a flight of locusts, mowing down the grass as they passed; but as long as the Haught herds plodded on, a way was made before them.

When the sun was sinking low, Beau shot a rabbit and broiled it on a stick, but while he was eating a horseman appeared and rode slowly towards his camp. He was coming in from the direction of Las Cruces, riding a black horse, nobly caparisoned; a tall man with a Mexican outfit, wearing an old-fashioned buckskin jacket. On his head was a low-crowned sombrero, he had a rifle under his knee, and when he rode up nearer Beau stood beside his horse, for his experience with Butch Hardigan had made him wary.

"Good evening, sir," greeted the Mexican, removing his hat, "can you tell me whose cattle those are? I am Manuel Duran de Chaves, of Las Cruces, and my people are becoming alarmed."

"Yes," responded Beau, "they are the herds of Henry Haught and his family, on their way to Arizona."

"Then they will have to turn back," sighed Duran. "The stage has not crossed this week. Since the snow began to melt in the high mountains of Colorado the Rio Grande has been flowing bank high."

"And is there no other way of crossing the river?"

"In two hundred miles," said Duran de Chaves, "there are only two fords, and the other one is quite impassable. So I fear that your friends — if they are your friends — will have to stay in this country. With so many good places to go I do not understand why they should come here where, as you see, it is nothing but desert."

"They are not my friends," replied Beau. "In fact, half the clan are my enemies, as you can see by looking at my head."

He touched the white rag with which his scalp was bound up, and Duran stepped off his horse.

"Your name is not unknown, Mr. McCutcheon," he said. "In fact it is spoken in two languages — *Cabeza Sangre* in Spanish and *Bee-tze-diltch*, by the Apaches. You are the Texan named Bloody Head, who fought so bravely against the Comanches and received such a blow from a war club. You have been waiting at Deep Lake for your wound to heal up, but it appears to me to be worse."

"Yes," admitted Beau, "I hurt it again in a fight that I had with Ash Haught. But how do you know what the Indians call me?"

"That is my business," replied Duran de Chaves, mysteriously. "I have to know what is going on. The price of cattle has risen to twenty dollars a head; and the Mexicans, as you know, raise cattle. I myself raise cattle, which is why it is so important to find out the truth in this affair. But the few Americans I met while watching the trail were the cowboys of Michael O'Grady, and they will tell me nothing. Except that Mr. Haught had better keep going if he wants to escape further trouble.

"But how can they keep going when, at the Crossing of the Rio Grande, a good horse can hardly swim across? It is a violent river, Mr. McCutcheon, and these Haughts are traveling with wagons. They cannot ferry them across, because our boat has been carried away; so what I expect is that the Haughts will stop over and, perhaps, eat all our grass."

"Very likely," agreed Beau, "they are no friends of mine. But you are a long way from home, Mr. Duran, and you must be a little hungry. Won't you have a piece of my rabbit?"

"With pleasure, my friend," replied Duran. "I see that you have been around, and a barnful of corn is nothing — at home — to half a tortilla, right here."

He accepted a leg of the rabbit; and then, as an after thought, drew out a pouch of parched corn and shared it with the Texan.

"Here is a little *pinole*," he said, "some ground corn mixed with panoche sugar. With a bag of this I can travel for days, but I thank you for the meat. If you will ride back with me to Las Cruces, I will give you some very good coffee. Your friends are going to water their cattle at the river that flows through Tularosa; and then, perhaps, they will camp for the night, though I would not advise it, myself. The people at Tularosa are very jealous of their rights, and the cattle will feed off their range. But every day has its end, and you look a little tired and worn."

"My head hurts me," replied McCutcheon, "and I slept out last night without food. So, with your permission, I will ride on to Las Cruces —"

"You are very welcome," answered Duran, who seemed to be built of steel and corded rawhide. "And, since you mention it, I slept out myself, without having the good fortune to kill a rabbit. But tell me about these Haughts, since we are both following after them. They came from the Brazos, did they not? And when their neighbors followed along to steal their cattle they hung sixteen of them by their horse-hobbles."

"Eighteen," corrected Beau. "But Captain Hightower told me that he thought they were fully justified. Some of these Texans, as you know, will steal anything. But not Jack Hightower. He is honest."

"Yes, he is honest," sighed Duran. "But he has brought all these Texans upon us, so I cannot say I am glad he has come. Where he goes they will follow and steal all our cattle. Yet I see you are riding one of his horses. How do I know? By this brand — HT on the left hip. That shows he is your friend. There is nothing so good as to ride a friend's horse when going into a strange country. But these ignorant officers up at Lincoln were ready to arrest you, anyway."

"Yes," agreed McCutcheon. "I do not know why, but I think there is some reward. But this horse I am riding was given to me by Captain Hightower himself."

"So I hear," nodded Duran. "But the brand does not show, and these officers are not really cattlemen. They cannot read brands, as the Mexicans can, but must burn a Long Rail from ears to tail to keep their cows from being stolen. And they so cut their ears that one half stands up and the other half hangs down, so that in a herd they can always be seen. But does this absurd-looking Jingle-bob save its owner's cattle? Does the Long Rail keep the cow from being stolen? No, and for a very good reason. He cannot hire men enough to brand them.

"They will drink, they will ride, they will cut every herd that passes; but Martin Hockaday is always shorthanded, and there is no one to brand his stock. Have you seen Jesse Mowbray and his band of cowboys, every man dressed in black velvet, with pearl-handled pistols on his hips? Last year they rode for *him*, trimming every herd of cattle that passed. Then they quit in a body and went to work for O'Grady. They are warriors. All they know is to fight. But your friend Captain Hightower is an honest man and a smart one. He does not need to steal other men's cows. Only it was a sad day for the Mexicans when he drove that first herd to the Pecos. Because, before they get through, they will have all our range and perhaps steal all our cows.

"To me it means little, since I have a store, a hotel, a mill to grind up our corn; but my people are not rich, they have little to lose and they do not like to be treated like slaves. They settled this country first, they fought off the Indians and brought in other people to do the work. But not the Duran de Chaves. For two hundred years they have led the way in battle. They are brave —

100

they will admit no defeat. A hundred to one, they would fight off the Navajos, any time! Or the Apaches, the Utes, the Comanches! At Cebolleta a colony of thirty families fought off five thousand Navajos for years. And when we were not fighting we would trade with them. Then organize a big party and march into their country, kill the warriors and bring home the women and children.

"When a young man wished to marry he would give his intended a woman for a slave; and so kindly did they treat them that the slaves would marry some warrior, who ran away to join them and raise a family of his own. But no man could live in Cebolleta who turned his back in battle. No matter what the odds, they must stand up and fight; and more than once my distinguished uncle, Don Manuel Duran de Chaves, would count out a pouch of bullets, one for every man, and lay them close to his hand. The first man to turn his back knew that Manuel would kill him, for he had a fine rifle and never missed. But perhaps, Mr. McCutcheon, I am keeping you too long, while I recite the brave deeds of my *parientes*? All is peace and quiet now, the Apaches respect me and never come to Las Cruces on their raids. But how to meet these Texans, who are swarming into our country! But I forget — you are a Texan, yourself."

"Only as Captain Hightower is a Texan," replied Beau. "He came from Virginia and joined the Texas Rangers. But the one man he hates is a cow-thief."

"Then I, too, am like him," responded Duran. "I do not find it necessary to steal. It is only the *pelados*, the

101

lower classes among my people who descend to stealing a cow. But come, let us be on our way. That is a very good horse that the Captain gave you. Did he send you into this country?"

"Well — maybe," answered Beau. "If it is any of your business."

"It is," answered Duran de Chaves, smiling. "I am sheriff of Doña Ana County."

CHAPTER
FOURTEEN

At Three Rivers

"It is a good thing," observed Duran de Chaves, "that you are seen riding into town with me. I and my brother have been sheriffs in Las Cruces for nearly twenty years. We take turns in holding office, since the New Mexican law will not permit me to serve all the time. So for two years I am sheriff and Pedro attends to our business — our store, our cattle and hotel. Then we change places and I run the business while Pedro runs the County.

"It is only a small County, since Lincoln has been cut off, and the Apaches make us no trouble. When they fight with the soldiers they do not come down here, to kill our herders and run off our sheep. They call me 'Don Manuel' and tell me everything that goes on. That is how I know just exactly what Butch Hardigan pays to hire the cowboys to bring in the steers. Five dollars a head and fifty cents for unbranded mavericks. He hangs those hides on the fence.

"But when the Colonel in command at Fort Stanton comes to make his official tour of inspection everything is perfectly regular. Major O'Grady was discharged from the service by Colonel Chevalier, who is honest,

103

so he moved down to Lincoln, elected Haley sheriff and took entire charge of the County. Then he hired Hockaday's cowboys, to run his Seven Rivers ranch for him, and sells his cattle to Butch Hardigan. But last year the circuit judge was murdered while on his way to Lincoln and Judge Brinton has refused to hold court there.

"He insists upon having all the trials in English, which the Spanish-speaking people cannot understand; so I have been compelled to summon a full panel of Americans from the cowboys along the river, and if you settle in this County I shall be very glad to summon you for the full fall term of the court. The witness fees are considerable. I receive ten cents a mile for mileage and several of the settlers are very glad indeed to attend court, with all expenses paid. It will be a good way also for you to gain information regarding the cattle-stealing that is undoubtedly going on."

"I will take it into consideration," promised Beau, "if I happen to locate in the County. Are the Americans easy to handle?"

"Almost too easy," replied Duran. "When their cattle have been shipped and there is nothing else to do they come and live in town. But they make a joke of half the cases in court and have very little respect for the law. Still, the Government insists that every case shall be tried in English, and I have to take whatever Americans I can get. Since the death of Judge Fountain, who was killed in the White Sand here, Judge Brinton has held court in Las Cruces, and my hotel is crowded with witnesses and officers of the law. It makes a nice vacation for the boys along the river, who otherwise would be short of cash."

"I believe I'm going to like this town," exclaimed Beau as they rode into Las Cruces after dark; and from the river below he could hear the water roaring as the sand passed over the bar. There would be no crossing for the Haughts' herds and wagons, as a rider had learned during the night, and, without attempting to cross, the cattle turned back and made their slow way to the north. Past Alamagordo and Tularosa they went at a swinging walk and at nightfall they settled down at Three Rivers, where the water came down from the peaks.

It was the end at last of their long journey across the desert in search of another range. A barren land, covered with greasewood and mesquite, set off by the black bulk of the lava beds, flanked by towering hills to the west. Between them and these cliffs there was a waste of level land — the White Sands, for which the valley was famous — a desert upon which a jack rabbit could hardly live but covered with coarse grass toward the north.

The White Sands were pure gypsum, drifting forty feet high whenever the wind swept in, but anchored at the base by tall yuccas and scraggly salt-bushes and rank-growing *sacaton* grass. Not a place to build a home but good enough for raising cows, and the Haughts had been driven far enough. From the Brazos to the Pecos they had fought their way, dragging their white covered wagons behind; but even on this desert there were people before them, who planned to drive them away.

Butch Hardigan, the horse-faced Irishman who sold beef to the Government at Fort Stanton, was watching them from the heights, and he claimed this range for his own. Up the canyon there was water, flowing down from the peaks, and, at Carrizozo, Major O'Grady still ran cattle. Not many — it was too far from Hockaday's vast herds and he had moved to Seven Rivers at the south — but it still was part of his range. His old range, almost deserted, but he claimed it for his own.

When his velvet-clad warriors rode back for their instructions he spoke quickly and to the point.

"Roust them out," he ordered and the range war was on, even though the Haughts did not know it.

Turned back by the river, avoided at the Ruidoso, their herd trimmed by Hockaday's Long Rail boys, they parked their wagons in a circle on the flat and set a double guard for the night. Out on the white sands they held their herds of cattle and waited for the storm to break. They were not welcome, that they knew, though their road had been cleared of every cow. It was just to get rid of them that the trail had been kept open. The cattle were up in the hills. But when they drifted down, mixing in with the trail-herds, the Haughts knew their troubles would begin.

"Ride 'way out around 'em," ordered Colonel Haught; and the women kept close to the wagons.

In a country like that, without a house in twenty miles and without a cowboy in sight, there would seem to be room for all, but through the first night the

Haughts rode their rounds, swinging far out to turn back their enemies. And, out in the sandhills Beau and Duran slept fitfully, with nothing but *pinole* for food. But the watch had been too close, not a herd was stampeded, and they started for the mountains at dawn.

"Let them fight," said Manuel. "They are outside my county and Sheriff Haley knows how to handle them. When Texan fights Texan —"

"Then comes the tug of war," ended McCutcheon; but Duran did not understand.

"All I know," he said, "is that the Rio Grande has been my friend. It has turned back these Texans, forty miles from Las Cruces, and they cannot ford the river for a month. Now I will take you across the valley to the San Andres Mountains, where I have a place in mind where we can kill a maverick beef. From there you can look down without being observed and see everything that goes on. It is a stone house, by a spring, and you can take your horse inside, since the roof of the fort is gone. It was burned, a year ago, by a band of Apache Indians, but for you it will be perfectly safe. Only wear, when you go out, this piece of white cloth and they will know you are Bee-tze-diltch."

He passed Beau a white rag, to wrap around his head, and set out across the White Sands at a lope. The ground, most of the way, was moist and springy; they rode around the patches of sand; and when they reached the other side they fell into a narrow canyon that led up to a rocky pass.

"This trail," explained Duran, "is the war-trace of the Mescaleros, when they pass over the San Andres to the north. Or to the west, as far as that goes, and down over the Jornada del Muerto to Las Cruces. It is ninety miles without a drop of water, along the steep banks of the Rio Grande, and for that reason it is called the Journey of the Dead, after a poor fellow who tried to cross it. When he reached the other end his body was so thin that they truly thought him a dead man. Yet to a man on a horse it is no journey at all — just a little ride before breakfast. And that reminds me, we will kill a yearling at the pass and you can hang it up in the shade. Only do not go out for a couple of days while I send a runner to the chief. Hosteen Tla is his name — Left-handed Man — and he would like a little present when he comes."

"I will give him some tobacco," promised Beau, and they toiled on up the steep heights. The San Andres Mountains are built up layer after layer, like a cake, with a crack down the middle at the pass; and at the top of the canyon there is a big spring of water, where wild cattle come down to drink. Duran killed a yearling, they hung it up in the shade and broiled it piece by piece on a forked stick.

"This house," said Manuel, "was built by a man named Johnson, who intended to run cattle on the west plains; but he was afraid of the Indians and drove them away from the water. So they killed him, and burned the house. You must get some little presents and I will send you up some food, for the Indians are always hungry when they go by here. But when they know who you are they will be very glad to greet you, for already they have heard of Bloody Head. The man who struck your head with a war club was a Comanche chief and when Leopard Coat killed him, the Apaches, who were looking on, gave you a name. Always wear a white rag when you go among them and tell them you are Cabeza Sangreta.

"I will tell the *Comancheros*, the Mexicans who trade with the Comanches, that you are a brave man and the friend of Hightower and they will not do you any harm. To be killed by such a man is held an honor among the Indians, who rather expect to get killed anyway; but they cannot understand why a man should be afraid, since we all must pass out, sooner or later. But my uncle, Don Manuel Duran de Chaves, was braver than them all, and I have learned to fight like him. I remember one time — but I will tell the story later, since you are interested in my people. Many of them are of the old *sangre azul*. The blood of warriors is in their veins.

"But the low Texans whom we meet think the Mexicans are all the same — only fit for cleaning stables and chopping wood. And yet they will fight, in their way. They have learned from the Comanches to draw their guns and charge, and the Indians are afraid of the smoke. Had they guns as good as we have — but enough, I must be gone. By this time tomorrow a man will come with five burros and bring you a load of food. You may pay him two dollars, if you will, for his services, and I will charge the rest to your account. Is there anything else you want? I have a store full of supplies, as you know, and anything I have is yours."

"Then do me a favor," smiled McCutcheon, "since I must stay here alone for days. Send me out some books to read. Have you any book written by William Shakespeare?"

"Shakespeare?" repeated Duran. "I have heard the name somewhere, but I cannot recall what he wrote. No, we have none, but I can send off and get you some. Just write the names on a paper. There is one book we do have, and I know it is excellent. *Don Quijote de la Mancha*, by Don Miguel de Cervantes Saavedra. It is written in Spanish, of course —"

"Then send it out," said Beau. "I will have a chance to brush up on my language. You speak English so well that —"

"Ah, thank you a thousand times," answered Duran, riding off. "I am glad to practice with the words. Until tomorrow, then, my friend, and I hope you find the one you seek. The lady, who is with the Haughts. Yes, at your age there is always a lady."

He laughed as McCutcheon began to blush, and galloped away down the trail.

CHAPTER
FIFTEEN

Sergeant Miles

Without waiting for the two days to pass, when he would be safe from Indian attacks, Beau rode around the point and gazed out across the western plains. The trail that led across it had been named the Journey of the Dead Man. Many men had died there, with water but a few miles away, for it was confined at the bottom of the canyon. Yet the broad mesa was green with grass and flowers, with mesquite trees, greasewood and yuccas; and the trail to his spring was worn deep by wild cattle, who found shelter on the wooded heights.

Except for the passing Indians it was an ideal place to live — the only sweet water in miles. Before the Apaches killed him, Johnson had built a cedar corral, around the spring, just down the canyon. But he had driven away the Indians, after they had used the water for centuries, and an arrow had ended his life. Now his homestead lay waiting for the next man to take a chance on it, and McCutcheon posted his notices.

From the edge of the cliffs that night Beau could see the fires that blazed in the guarded Haught camp; and there, standing beside one of them, was Musette herself, though she did not know he was watching.

Never since that night when he had struck back at Ash and fought him until the stampede shook the earth; never since that night had he seen the little girl who had taken him for her knight. Out of the rush of cattle at Horsehead Crossing she had entered into his life — her mare bucking, dragged by one foot — and with the pistol he always wore he had shot the horse down and taken her into his arms. Then a rough hand had slapped him over, Mrs. Haught had struck him aside, and he had ridden off after Hightower's herd. Then the Comanches rode out on them, there was a swift whirl of racing horses, and Beau had charged into their midst. That was the way his father had taught him — never to wait, to fear nothing, and to go for the nearest man. It was the way of the Texas Rangers learned from Sam Houston and Jack Hays and the rest of that impetuous band.

It was Hightower's way, though he was not born in Texas, and in a fight he always noticed those in front. That was why he had seen McCutcheon and charged in to help him. It was why Beau was working for him now. There were other Texans as brave, but not all of them were as honest, and Captain Jack was looking for his kind. He wanted men he could trust in that tumult of fighting and stealing, in that welter of mavericks, running wild without a brand. That was why McCutcheon was staying at Johnson's canyon with his head wrapped up in a rag.

But below, at last, they had come to rest — Musette and the whole family of Haughts — and there was one Haught already who wanted to marry her. Some cousin, for they kept within the clan. A turbulent lot, quick to take up a quarrel; but Hightower had decided they were honest. Honest among themselves, though they had hung eighteen neighbors. But still, as cowmen went, they were square. Ash was the fighting one, who had learned to shoot left-handed, so he would not get a bullet through his heart.

He had had his head battered twice in one day, and once by Beau McCutcheon. And Beau was still wearing a rag over his wound, for Ash had hit him hard. He had sent word to Beau the next day to keep away from Musette and McCutcheon knew he meant it. But with the Lincoln County boys on his trail, Ash would have enough fighting to do. Major O'Grady had fought the Apaches for three years himself, and his warriors had been picked, to a man. They were making big money and they knew their business, which was to move strange outfits off the range. Move them quick, before they got located — and the second night they started a stampede.

Beau was still out on the cliff, looking down across the wide valley at the twinkling fires of the camp when, without the least warning, every cow at once, the Haught cattle rose up and flew. There was some way of starting them, learned perhaps from the Apaches, that put them all on the jump. They poured out across the valley with a roar like the clatter-gates of hell, turning to the right as the Haught cowboys took after them and headed them through the white sands. Then, halfway to the Ruidoso, the pistols began to pop and Beau knew the battle was on.

When the shooting was over the cattle were still running, but at last they came to a stop. At dawn they were toiling back again through that ocean of drifting sand, and an Indian was riding up the trail. His stunted pony was shod with rawhide horseshoes that clung to the rocks as he came on, but when he saw this white man, with a rag around his head, calmly waiting at the head of the trail he halted and held up his hand.

"How," he said, whipping closer. "*Bueno!*"

That was to say: 'Good!' He came good.

"Don Manuel say you good man!" he continued. "Cabeza Sangre, no?"

"Yes," answered Beau, holding up his hand for peace. And he beckoned him on to the house. Then he pointed to the beef, where it hung in the corner, and the Indian cut off a strip. He cooked it, saying nothing, in the abandoned fireplace, shook hands and rode away. When a Mexican came in at noon he looked at the horse-tracks and shrugged.

"Apache," he said, stepping down from his burro; and glanced up at the peaks as he spoke.

"Scare cows?" asked McCutcheon, pointing down into the valley where the scattered cattle were being driven back, and the Mexican shrugged again.

"*Quien sabe,*" he grunted. "Who knows?"

Here was an answer to the mysterious stampede, so similar to the one at Deep Lake. At the smell of an Indian, coming down the wind, every cow-brute had leaped to its feet. It was explanation enough for Beau, who had seen Comanche stampedes before, and he went on unpacking the loads. Then he brewed a pot of coffee, motioned the Mexican to drink, and stacked up his provisions by the fireplace.

"*Comido*," he said, and watched old Juan eat while he looked through the collections of books. They were all in Spanish, and he picked a worn one up.

"Ha!" he exclaimed. "*Don Quijote!*"

"Yes, yes," responded Juan. "A good book. Very old. The story of Don Quijote and his squire, Sancho Panza. The only book Don Manuel will read. He says that reading is bad for the eyes, and it is necessary for him to shoot straight."

"A thousand thanks," answered McCutcheon. "Here is a letter for your *patron*. Please ask him to mail it for me and I will wait till I hear from my boss."

"To be sure," replied Juan and, with a last sip of coffee, he started off down the trail.

Beau was still in the stone house — where he could look out the broken window and see anyone coming up the trail — when he jumped up and reached for his gun. Up the trail — and he knew him — was his pet horse, Hot Foot, who had borne him so fast and far when he rode away from Fort Davis. And, riding on his back, was Rye Miles, leaning forward and looking for tracks. But behind him was Captain Hightower.

McCutcheon stepped out, smiling, though his heart was in his mouth, and Miles regarded him grimly.

"Sergeant Miles," said Hightower, spurring forward, "shake hands with Beau McCutcheon."

"Glad to meet you, sir," answered Miles, without shaking hands. "Are you the man that stole my horse?"

"We sent him right back, Rye," defended Jack, "as soon as we found a man we could trust. With a horse as good as that, and heading towards the Line, it wouldn't pay to take any chances."

"Well — no," agreed the Ranger. "With those *hombres* we saw when we went through Lincoln I was lucky to get him back at all. Never mind about petting him, Mr. McCutcheon, if you don't mind. I'm mighty particular about that horse. Best animal I ever rode and I sure took it hard when you had the nerve to grab him that night. But the Captain explained that it was all a mistake and — well, all right!" and he shook hands.

"Now, boys," began Hightower, "I've left a big herd of cattle to get you located and started on this work. The Cattlemen's Association have decided to spare no expense. There were two men killed last night in the first scrimmage with the Haughts and the Seven Rivers boys were whipped off. But this is only the beginning. They've got a big bunch of warriors, the profits are good and Sheriff Haley runs the town. I want you to find out who is starting these stampedes and co-operate with the Haughts all you can."

"That's easy," replied Beau. "They're started by an Indian named Hosteen Tla — and the sheriff of Doña Ana, Manuel Duran, will take care of him. But who the hell can co-operate with that Haught outfit —"

"Leave 'em to me," spoke up Rye Miles, confidently. "I'll tame 'em. They made the mistake of stepping across the line from Lincoln County, where the whole damned Government is crooked, but what are the Rangers for?"

"They are to straighten out," said Hightower, "just such feuds as this before they result in bloodshed, and it's my opinion there'll be war in a month, and I'm going to send for two more men. Get the jump on 'em at the start, before these killings begin —"

"They've done started already," objected Miles. "Two men killed last night, and both Seven) Rivers warriors. But I'm going right over there and throw in with these Haughts and —"

"Anyway you please, Rye," agreed Hightower pacifically. "But don't think for a minute it will be easy. These are the same Haughts that hung eighteen neighbors with horse-hobbles —"

"That's all right," came back Miles, "they needed hanging. As long as the Haughts are honest it's O.K. with me, as old Stonewall Jackson used to say. The circuit judge is coming to Lincoln next month and I'm going to make some arrests."

"There's a young lawyer in Lincoln that will handle our cases," remarked Hightower, looking out the window. "But what cattle are these, Beau, that are coming in to water? And not a single cow branded! That's the greatest single cause of all this stealing — these mavericks roaming the plains. Martin Hockaday is going to find it is absolutely impossible to keep his cattle branded at all. Because, with these Texas trail herds going out and a good market in the north, he can't keep his men a month. All they've got to do is slap their brand on every maverick and sell it for twenty dollars.

117

"Now, Beau," said the Captain, "the first thing I want you to do is trap these wild cattle and brand them. You can contribute a dollar a head to the association if you want to, but we can talk that over later. And if any cows come in that have got a Texas brand on them, seize them and send them out to the first herd going through and we'll pay half what you get to the owners. That's what Martin Hockaday is supposed to do, but he never keeps any books. Just grabs them and keeps the money and you can't blame him too much, the way these rustlers are trimming him. But, when it's too late, he's going to regret this. Raising the damdest bunch of cow-thieves the world has ever seen, and they're getting worse all the time. Red Ryan will stop a team of oxen, slap the Fence Rail on their ribs and turn them out on the range. And if the Mexicans make any protest he'll burn a Fence Rail on their rump and jingle-bob their ears. That boy is a bad one — a good-hearted kid, but with no more principles than a rattlesnake.

"As long as he's running wild there's going to be trouble. That's all, Beau. Be careful, Rye. And never forget you're a Ranger."

CHAPTER
SIXTEEN

Every Man a General

"You heard him," said Miles, as Hightower rode away, "but with the Rangers every man is a general. Go ahead and trap your mavericks, if you want to. I'll ride over and see that Haught outfit."

He poured out some corn to feed Hot Foot, broiled a strip of beef on a stick and rode off without saying good-by. Rye was a man of action, six feet tall and built in proportion, with a shock of bristling red hair that stood out under his hat like a halo. His eyes were steel blue, with that deceptively mild look that so often goes with his kind; until the time for action came and then his good humor was gone. He had not forgiven Beau McCutcheon, even yet, for riding off on his horse; and when he came back, late at night, he lit a fire and broiled some beef, saying nothing.

"Why the hell didn't you tell me she was there?" he asked at last; and Beau laughed and looked away.

"I knew you'd see her," he said. "Isn't she the prettiest little girl you ever saw in your life?"

"Little!" exclaimed Miles, stopping to stare. "She's five foot ten if she's an inch. The finest-looking woman I ever saw, but she could pole-axe a bull with one hand.

Say, who is this Barney Hoops who thinks he's so important? I damned near had a fight with him at the start. He followed me to my horse and tried to warn me off — said Odette was his girl, and all that, but —"

"Oh," broke in Beau. "You mean Odette!"

"W'y, sure I mean Odette. Who else could I mean? So I told Mr. Hoops I'd wait for *her* to say it and —"

"Didn't you see Musette?" clamored Beau. "A little girl with brown eyes and lots and lots of dark hair and —"

"Oh — her!" grunted Miles. "That little girl? She was sitting over there with her grandmother and never said a word. But just when I went to go she slipped a note in my pocket and, so help me God, you could've knocked me down with a feather, she had such a look in her eye. Then this Barney Hoops followed after me and — well, here's your note. I'm eating."

He reached into his leather vest above the two pistols that swung so handy at his hips and as Beau looked at the note he closed his eyes and sighed.

"Well, what does it say?" demanded Miles and McCutcheon handed it over.

"'It is the lark and not the nightingale,'" muttered Rye, and passed it back impatiently. "What's a nightingale?" he asked.

"Oh, it's a bird," explained Beau.

"Yes, but what does it mean?" insisted Miles. "And why did she pass it to me? I thought for a minute that I'd made a winning with both of them when I only wanted one, she had such a look in her eyes. And then this Barney Hoops, that had been watching for his chance, had the nerve to warn me away from her. From Odette, I mean, and him a big, fat slob — but a fighting man, I reckon — and that's the only reason I didn't hit him. All the other men were out, standing guard over the herd, but he had plenty of time. All the time there was, and I noticed in particular how he never took his eyes off of *her*. And she sitting there so innocent, as if she never saw him. He's some relation, I reckon."

"Second cousin on her mother's side. What did you think of Mrs. Haught?"

"A holy terror. I could see that from the start. They were all sitting around the fire, when I rode in and Barney Hoops jumped up. He was a kind of a guard, I reckon — asked me my business and everything — but I never got a chance to tell him anything. Because every woman there knew Hot Foot, and they all asked where *you* were. That's something I never do is let women pet my horses, but when *she* came over, just as smiling and confident, and rubbed him on the nose — Well, I looked into her eyes, and they're a violet blue —"

"Did Musette ask for me?" demanded Beau.

"She might've," responded Miles. "There were so many of them talking I never noticed. Those women hadn't seen a man for a month — except their own kin, of course — and I answered them all at once. Then the old lady, Elvina, took the floor and I couldn't get a word in edgewise. First she told about naming all her children. A fortune-teller had advised her that her lucky names would all end with *ette*. Odette, Musette, Jeanette and all the rest of them, and her son's lucky name ended in *elles*. She called him Ashheels — he was a famous Greek fighting man — but I never even heard of him.

"Then she began to talk about this terrible Red Ryan, and what a bad man he was, and I said Red had come in with my pardner, when he made his escape from Fort Davis. That set 'em all off — you must have insulted Musette —"

"I did not," denied Beau. "She's the sweetest little girl in the world and old Gram took her out to see me —"

"Well, anyhow, this Red Ryan got gay with Odette and she slapped him over backwards —"

"Yes, I know," broke in McCutcheon, "but what did you find out, anyway?"

"I found out," answered Miles, "that we're going to have neighbors. The Haughts have had a bunch of Mexicans, mixing mud and molding adobe bricks; and in another week's time they'll have a regular fort, with a big oak gate and everything. Then they'll all move inside and if I want to see Odette —"

He wandered on and Beau almost stopped listening to him, he was so interested to hear from Musette. His little girl was there and he was still her brave knight. She was still reading Shakespeare and talking about Romeo and Juliet, though Rye had never heard of them.

Miles jumped up on his horse and went racing across the mesa, and when he came back it was in the company of Manuel Duran.

"Good morning," greeted Don Manuel. "I have brought out some books for you, and Mr. Miles has been so kind as to tell me about Henry Haught, who is building a fort down at Three Rivers. That is out of my county, but his cattle will range inside of it; and I was wondering if he would object if we levied a nominal assessment."

"Oh, are you the sheriff?" inquired Miles, as Beau accepted the books; and half an hour later, when he looked up from his reading, they were talking about fighting Apaches.

"This is Manuel Duran," said Rye. "Of the most famous fighting Durans of New Mexico. His uncle was a Colonel in the Civil War, after Armijo had quit, and Don Manuel tied into Colonel Price lone-handed with about a thousand New Mexicans, and ran him out of the state. W'y, hell, he's got these Apaches so badly licked they're afraid to come down out of the hills. Unless they get his personal permission."

"Yes, I know," answered Beau. "Their chief was through here yesterday and ate a bellyful of meat, and I noticed how respectful he was. Tell him the next time he comes, Don Manuel, to bring his wife along and stay awhile. I want him to ask her to make a buckskin suit for a little lady I know. And tell him I'll pay for it, handsomely. Would fifty dollars be enough?"

"Oh, plenty — if he likes you," smiled Manuel. "Have you found your girl, at last? The Indian women, as you know, are afraid of American men; but if you will allow him to bring *two* of his wives —"

"Fine," laughed McCutcheon. "And I will ask him to take them over to Haught's fort, to fit the little lady, Miss Musette Haught."

"I will do so," promised Duran. "After a few days have elapsed, of course. I am informed by my *mozo*, Juan, that he had seen Tla's tracks by your spring, and that you understood what his errand had been. Jesse Mowbray hired him — I am sure you understand — but it will never happen again, because two of Jesse's men were killed. So, after a few days, I will send Tla over here and you can give him a little meat. But be sure to give him an unbranded animal or Mr. Hardigan will object. He has the Government contract, you know, to keep these Indians in beef; but I am afraid that Mr. Hardigan does not feed them very well. For, though he is paid on issue day for feeding fifteen hundred Apaches, there are never more than seven hundred, and even then he never has enough."

Don Manuel smiled easily as he stepped down from his horse but, just before he left, he inquired if Red Ryan was in the employ of Captain Hightower.

"I might just as well tell you," he said, "that we had a visit from Ryan last week, with a company of ten or twelve warriors, as he calls them. A band of Comanches had driven off several hundred steers from the herd of a Texas trail-man, and when the Americans under Ryan came upon them they were down below Las Cruces, disposing of their cattle to a band of *comancheros*, which is the name we have for the Mexican traders who exchange beads and sugar for beef.

"These *comancheros* are known to the Comanches," he went on, "who for many years have raided into Texas; and, although it is dangerous, they go out to meet them and trade them blankets and whisky. Or perhaps a few rifles, a little ammunition — I do not know for myself. They are a low class of *pelados*, but brave, or they would not venture out there; and when Ryan and his men rode up on them they had a little fight. Three Indians were killed — one Mexican, also — and the Americans took all the cattle. But whether they delivered them to Martin Hockaday is something I do not know."

"They did not," spoke up Miles. "I was through Deep Lake only yesterday and Red Ryan had just come in. But he did not bring in the steers. Just the scalps of three Comanches —"

"Ah! Aha!" shrugged Don Manuel; and he galloped away down the trail.

CHAPTER
SEVENTEEN

A Lawyer

"These warriors," observed Miles, "are all the same. They trim every herd for mavericks and strays and then they turn around and steal the strays themselves, though I hadn't heard about the *comancheros*. But Jesse Mowbray and his men operate at Seven Rivers, which is halfway down the Pecos towards El Paso. I wonder if, by any chance, they are buying beef from Red."

"Don't think so," replied Beau. "They're working for Major O'Grady and he's trying to keep things to himself. But when he tackled the Haught boys they were a little too much for him, although Hosteen Tla is scared out."

"I went over there," volunteered Miles at last, "with the idea of putting in with them, but the only man I saw was Barney Hoops and he wasn't very friendly. The way I look at it, we've got to have some fighting men and the Haught boys are reasonably honest. We could use them, Beau, if we ever had a run-in and had to take on Jesse Mowbray. But I want to know what Red Ryan is up to before I make another move. Except to see

Odette, of course. I can't let this Barney run it over me."

"No indeed!" agreed McCutcheon. "And while you're about it —"

"You steal your own girl!" bantered Miles. "The Captain would give us hell, if he knowed. A Texas Ranger ain't supposed to have a wife. Or a home or nothing else. He's supposed to ride around all over the state of Texas, being transferred as soon as he's known, but when I meet a girl like Odette —"

"Or Musette," added Beau; and they laughed.

Rye worked a little while, helping Beau brand up the mavericks, but in about an hour he rode off down the trail and didn't come back for four days.

"What do you think now?" he asked. "A band of Comanches raided Deep Lake last night and ran off every horse they've got. And before Red Ryan had his men remounted they were halfway to the Guadelupes. They were Comanches, I know, because they used a knotted reata to saw their way through that adobe corral. Cut out a big section and passed the horses through, one at a time. The ground was stomped flat with moccasin tracks and there wasn't an Apache *tewa* in the bunch. The moon was just past the full, too, and there wasn't a chance to ketch up on them.

"But Martin Hockaday was good and mad — he lost a hundred and fifty-four horses — and he'd just found out where they take them. Away down on the Rio Grande, below Las Cruces, where those Mexican *comancheros* hang out. Red had traced the Comanches right to them; so, instead of trailing them to the

127

Guadelupes from Deep Lake, Martin enlisted a big bunch of buffalo-hunters that was going through and started down to make a clean-up. Grab every Comanche cow that had a Texas brand on it, and use his powers of attorney. The old zinc pipe is tied on the back of his saddle and Martin has got blood in his eye. He's even wearing his six-shooters; and when he does that he means business."

He spilled out a feed of corn for Hot Foot, grabbed a sackful of jerked beef and set off without looking back and, after thinking it over, McCutcheon went on with his work. There was branding to do, someone had to do it; and Miles belonged to the Rangers, where every man was a general. He did not feel the need of any company, but headed off alone for Las Cruces.

Two days went by, there was a big dust to the south, and then an enormous herd of cattle came in sight, surrounded by American cowboys. This would be a great blow to Don Manuel and his people, who had been buying stolen cattle for years; but Hockaday had hung on his pistols and hired every cowboy on the Pecos. The cows came back in a long line, heading for the Ruidoso, and somewhere in the bunch was Rye Miles, who had been trained to be a general.

When he returned, without a doubt, he would have a tally of the whole herd, and he would claim them in the name of Texas. Martin Hockaday had been claiming them, but he never sent any back. Now the Cattlemen's Association had brought the law into the country. They were going to sell the steers to the first herd passing through, and send half the profits to the owners.

Everybody knew them — there were half the brands in Western Texas — but Hockaday never kept any books. And the rustlers were all stealing from *him*.

Jesse Mowbray was selling mavericks for five dollars a head to Butch Hardigan, and *he* was selling them to the Government. But an inspector had just counted Butch's Apaches and found less than seven hundred. Quite a difference between that and fifteen hundred; and the Mescaleros didn't like beef, anyway. They preferred horse-meat, and the Comanches had shown them how to get it.

Sergeant Miles had the feeling that he was making himself very unpopular when, at the end of the long drive, he introduced himself officially. And when he claimed the steers in the name of Texas he nearly started a riot. There were rustlers on the Pecos who had never heard of the law until Captain Hightower came into the country. He had started it all by refusing to accept the mixed herd that Lester and John had picked up on the open plains, and Hockaday was vexed.

After taking sixty men to Las Cruces and back; and nearly having a fight with the Mexicans, to have a man step in and claim the whole herd was something out of the ordinary. Still, Rye Miles had his papers from the Western Cattlemen's Association and he might have made good on his bluff had not another stranger stepped in. He was a little wisp of a man, with stooped shoulders and a visionary eye — a lawyer, in fact — and after a few words with Hockaday he stepped back and smiled.

129

"Your papers are all right, Mr. Miles," said Martin. "It was only under a great extremity that I undertook to seize these cattle at all. But I have just suffered the loss of every horse in my corral at the hands of these same Comanches, and when we arrived on the scene here were these Mexicans, half of them riding around on our mounts. The other half of the horses had been killed to provide a feast for the Comanches and, under the circumstances, I feel I am fully justified in taking all the stock."

"Sure is," chipped in Red Ryan. "And where do *we* come in? Ain't we got a legal claim to half these steers, for taking them away from the Injuns?"

"And gentlemen," suggested the lawyer, whose name was Sweeny, "I will call your attention to another fact, in regard to these powers of attorney. In no place is it specified *when* the cattle shall be sold and when the money shall be paid to the owners. And since, in this case, time is the essence of the contract —"

"I won't pay it, that's all," stated Hockaday. "I've been robbed once, back in Texas, by a gang of thieving lawyers, who took advantage of my signing a lot of papers to collect every dollar I had. I went bankrupt in Texas and came out to this country to get another start in life; and no lawyer — not even this one — is going to make me pay. Those notes and bills of sale that they're holding against me have been outlawed, years ago; and as long as I stay outside the state of Texas —"

"Three cheers!" bellowed Ryan, "for Martin Hockaday!"

And they all went in for a drink.

130

CHAPTER
EIGHTEEN

The Haughts Give Warning

"The lawyers," said Rye Miles, "will send this country to hell if somebody doesn't kill them off. That little shrimp is Bryan Sweeny, the one Hightower spoke of, over in Lincoln, and he's been tagging along for forty miles, just for the chance to get in a word. I heard him telling Hockaday that what he needed was a good, smart attorney, to look after his legal interests."

"'Keeping me out of jail,'" says Martin, "and he gave me a look when I rode off. They've got me spotted now for a Texas Ranger, and half of them are on the dodge. When I came by the Haught fort on my way home, this same Barney Hoops was standing at the door; and he waved me on, like this. They think you're an outlaw, of course."

"Did you see Musette?" asked Beau.

"No, nor Odette, either," grumbled Miles. "But I saw old Gram and chief Tla and his two wives, sitting in the shade when I passed and Gram, she waved her hand to me."

"Oh, I know!" cried Beau. "They're down measuring Musette for that buckskin suit I ordered. Gram's going to boss the job, and I gave Tla the fifty dollars."

"Well, where do *you* come in, buying clothes for Musette?" demanded Miles. "You must figure on getting married!"

"We do," nodded Beau. "As soon as she's sixteen, and she's going on fifteen now. She gave me a kiss and promised to wait for me, and right here is where we'll make our home. I've staked out a homestead already and —"

"Located the water?" inquired Miles. "I see you've branded all these cows. You're not so crazy as you look, Mr. McCutcheon, with your head all tied up in a rag. This is the only good spring in the country, too — the others are all alkali and gyp."

"Finest water in fifty miles," boasted Beau. "Did you see those Haught cattle down below? Just waiting for a chance to get a good drink — and all the other cows, too. Once they sneak in and get a good taste they'll always come back for more, and this mesa up here is covered with grass."

"Yes," observed Miles, sarcastically. "If the Indians don't kill you —"

"Old Tla is my friend," objected Beau. "He came over yesterday, and his old wife is going to make a dress. She says the young girl doesn't know how to work in buckskin, but she's a pretty little thing. Never looked up, the whole time she was here —"

"If you could only earn a living," went on Rye relentlessly, "you could almost afford to get married."

132

"Got that cinched, already," laughed McCutcheon. "Been summoned for a professional juryman. The new judge is very particular to have all these Mexicans barred. He's got some important cases coming up, when we crack down on these cow-thieves, and he wants only men that understand English. Then there's ten cents a mile mileage, for going to town and back, and expenses while I'm serving on the jury. With my hundred dollars a month as an underground agent, and all the mavericks I'm going to brand —"

"Well, you'll do," pronounced Miles, "until Captain Hightower gets back to town, and then he'll be sending you all over seven counties. But what are you going to do with Musette, when you get summoned to Las Cruces, to sit on those juries you spoke of?"

"I'll take her, too!" smiled McCutcheon. "That is, when we're married; and every time the Indians come through I'll tell them to help themselves to beef. They can't burn the house down, anyway; because it's been burned down once, already."

"Fair enough," laughed Miles. "But if you knew what I do, you wouldn't feel quite so good. When Red Ryan and his warriors left Deep Lake, they took half the stolen cattle with them, and when I went through Lincoln, Haley tried to hire me for five dollars a day. Professional gunman, and Butch Hardigan is hiring more, but I told them I was on my way. When they hear what I tried to pull on Martin Hockaday they'll run me out of town. I'm a marked man already, on account of my horse, but when they hear I'm working for Hightower — I believe I'll stay home for a while."

133

"All right," agreed Beau; and the next morning at daylight they were building a cattle-trap. It was just a gap in the corral, where the wild cattle could squeeze in between limber cedar poles, set sideways in the breach. They came down at night from the timbered peaks and, once inside, they were his. McCutcheon was busy with his branding-iron when Henry Haught and his son rode up, and they looked at the hot irons disdainfully.

"What's the matter?" demanded Haught. "Can't you boys throw a rope, or are you working Mexican style?"

"We're working Mexican style," answered Beau, and kept his eye on Ash.

"I notice," went on Haught, "jest as soon as I get settled, you start in branding cows. Moving in on me, like, but I warn you right now to leave my cattle *alone*."

"Our orders," spoke up Miles, "from the President of the Western Texas Cattlemen's Association, are to brand every calf in the iron of its mother and take all the mavericks for ourselves. Any objections to that?"

"None whatever," returned Henry Haught grimly, "as long as you do that; but our cows are coming up here to get a drink of water and be damned careful what you *do*. Because the first time I find a brand of mine altered —"

"Be careful what you say," warned McCutcheon, "or I'll bounce a stone off your head. And you Ash, I've been watching you, so don't reach for that gun unless you mean to use it."

"Never mind, now," retorted Haught. "We came up here peaceful, to see what these cattle were waiting for. Why don't you build a fence, if you want to keep them out, instead of baiting them into a trap. I know your record, young man —"

"Yes, and you know *mine*," replied Rye Miles, drawing his gun. "I'm a sergeant in the Texas Rangers. And by the way, I know *your* record."

He waved them away scornfully, but Henry Haught bristled back at him.

"My record is well known," he admitted. "But this isn't Texas, young man. I'm proud of what I did and I'd do it all over again. To cow-thieves. And, just to show you I mean it, I'm offering five hundred dollars reward for the arrest and conviction of any man caught stealing my cows."

"Good enough," answered the Ranger, "I'll try to remember that. But don't you think, Mr. Haught, you're taking a good deal for granted when —"

"I'm warning you!" shouted Haught, his voice trembling with passion. "I've lost three thousand head of cows since I came into this country and I warn you to stay away. And keep away from my daughters or —"

"Or what?" demanded Miles, boldly. "I'll call on your daughters whenever I damned please, and don't try to run any ranikaboos over *me*."

"Come on!" said Ash to his father, "before you get gun-shot by this tough *hombre*, here, Mr. McCutcheon. He's just waiting for the chance to plug you, and call it self-defense."

"I'm waiting for you to make a crooked move, if that's what you mean," answered Beau. "But if you can ever find a calf that I misbranded —"

"You don't need to misbrand calves," retorted Ash, "as long as you can find full-grown mavericks. You and your Captain Hightower, that's so honest he leans over backwards —"

"That'll do," warned Miles, "and you'd better be on your way before something happens to you. You've got plenty of people to fight, without coming clear up here. Red Ryan and his warriors have quit Martin Hockaday and —"

"They *have?*" yelped Ash Haught. "When?"

"Yesterday morning. Taking half Hockaday's Texas cattle!"

"We'll be going," decided Henry Haught, and started down the trail on the run.

"I think I'll go over and investigate that slaughter-house," murmured Miles, "while Butch Hardigan is away. Something tells me he'll have some other rat-killing to do that'll require his immediate attention."

CHAPTER
NINETEEN

A Little Hell of
Their Own

A posse of twenty men, armed with rifles and pistols and mounted on the best of horses, was gathered before Sheriff Haley's office, passing the bottles around. The work they had to do did not call for cold courage but rather the reckless kind, and Mexicans and Americans alike had set out to get *one man*.

He was an innocent-looking fellow, this J. Rogers Ismay, an Englishman, unaccustomed to the ways of the West but carried away by the love of adventure; and when Red Ryan had dropped in at his ranch on the Rio Feliz with a big herd of Texas cattle it seemed only the usual thing. He had known these doughty warriors who rode for Martin Hockaday, fighting off Indians and Texans alike when the occasion came to do so, and he had never seen one of them weaken.

And he had known the little lawyer, Bryan Sweeny, who did not fear even to oppose Major O'Grady. They had gone into business together, he and Ismay, drawing the trade from O'Grady's big store, and neither of them had experienced a tremor. Yet he knew, without thinking about it, that the Major owned the town, and that he was opposed to Sweeny and his policies. For Sweeny had had the effrontery to refuse a certain case on the ground that it was not honest — and O'Grady a man who had fought the Apaches, neither expecting nor giving quarter!

It was a hard formation, though Ismay did not know it, and he set off for Lincoln alone. But as he rode down the trail towards Lincoln he met these men who had been his friends and, before he could even ask them for a drink, one of them had shot him off his horse. They were drunk, of course, and they shot the horse too, although all they were instructed to do was to serve a writ of attachment. But twenty men were not called for to do the work of an attorney's clerk, and the posse understood. This Englishman had had the nerve to oppose O'Grady in everything, and the time had come for a showdown. There were getting to be too many men foolish enough to lay down their little deuce against the hand of a man who held aces, a man accustomed to rule by any means, fair or foul, and Sweeny had gone too far. He had solicited the legal practice of Martin Hockaday and won him over to the *law*. When everybody knew that O'Grady ruled the town, and the law had nothing to do with it.

Even Hockaday knew that much; but he had retained Sweeny, all the same, after his last bunch of warriors quit him. And Martin for years had been opposed to all lawyers, with their wise saws and legal verbiage, putting his trust in an old iron safe, named for some reason the Salamander safe. So far it had served him well — no one else knew the combination — but this last raid on his herds by the Western Texas Cattlemen's Association had made him lose his first faith. When he had been ready to weaken and even give back the branded steers, Sweeny had laid his finger on the essential weakness even of his powers of attorney.

These papers which he had treasured for years in his section of zinc water pipe — even flashing them on Henry Haught and stripping Haught's herd of every stray! Sweeny had revealed at a glance that they had no authority before the law, because they had not specified *when*. It was taken for granted that, after seizing the stolen steers, he would sell them and restore one-half to the distant, half-forgotten owners. But Red Ryan had shown him a higher law when he had driven half the herd away. He could have taken them all, but he rather admired this little lawyer who had the nerve to stand up to the Western Cattlemen's Association! So they left him half their herd, to see if he could keep them when Hightower came back with more men.

They were all hiring gunmen, and Hightower was hiring Rangers, men whose business it was to round up outlaws and shoot it out, man to man. Rye Miles had played a lone hand in the cause of the Association and the law, but Bryan Sweeny had raised his limber finger and put it on the spot. He had shown them that these powers of attorney were as nothing. They did not specify *when* the money was to be paid. That was the same as saying that they would never be paid, and Ryan saw his chance to quit.

He was going to quit, anyhow, but he had never for a minute expected that he could get away with it lawfully. A man like this lawyer would come in very handy if they ever had courts again; but since the death of Judge Fountain, the prosecuting attorney, who had been killed just before the former court, it looked as if they would revert to first principles:

"When they shall take who have the power
And they shall keep who can."

But when, the next day, they found J. Rogers Ismay, the Englishman, dead in the trail, they realized that the war was on.

Red Ryan and his warriors had been heading for Lincoln when they came upon Sweeny's partner, dead; and when they saw five of O'Grady's men in the distance they charged in like fighting Comanches. Two men split off from the rest and tried, as fellow outlaws, to make peace, but Red Ryan was implacable.

"No," he said, "you killed my pardner and laid him by his horse to make fun of him. Now tell me if you think *this* is funny."

He killed them both and took an oath to kill the rest of them — a large order, there were twenty of them — but before Red Ryan got through he had killed just twenty men. Not those particular men, but any others he happened to hit; and, while he was doing it, he made the law a joke in his easy, carefree way. Even the Governor of New Mexico couldn't persuade him to quit. He liked the game, once the pot had been opened, and he knew they would kill him anyway; so he shot these two men, just to show what he could do, and even Captain Hightower was thwarted.

For months he had seen this war coming on and had aroused the Association to move against it. They had sent in two men, and one of them a Ranger, but Martin Hockaday had spoiled it all. He had hired sixty gunmen, raided the Mexican settlements and seized every steer that had a Texas brand; but the men he had hired had turned against him and started a little hell of their own.

CHAPTER
TWENTY

The Battle

First they had sworn out warrants against each other, still clinging to a pretense of law, but the first two men were killed. They went on hiring gunmen, swearing out more warrants, recruiting ardent friends for the fray. But the last prosecuting attorney had been killed while going to court and nobody would take his place. The word was passed around that a conspiracy had been discovered to kill the judge on his bench and Judge Bristol would not come to Lincoln to open the circuit court.

The courtroom was at the top of a two-story building, the first floor being O'Grady's store; there was no jail worthy of the name; and if court was ever called, people felt morally certain that the meeting of the clans would start a war. At present all was quiet, although Sheriff Haley had offered a reward for Red Ryan, dead or alive, on account of the killing of two men. Whereas Ryan held Haley personally responsible for the shooting of his English friend Ismay.

Haley it was who had sent twenty men, all deputized, to serve a writ of attachment on Ismay's property, over on the Rio Feliz. They had shot him down without even a pretense of demanding that he should surrender, and as a joke they had laid him out beside the body of his horse, with his coat under his horse's head. This as a taunt for his friends who came after him; and then Red Ryan had killed two deputies.

But on the first of April, as the law required, they had decided to open, and then adjourn court. Sheriff Haley, with two deputies and the clerk of the court, climbed the narrow stairway, opened court and as promptly adjourned. But as they were walking down the road past Sweeny's store, six heads bobbed up from behind an adobe wall, six rifles opened fire, and Sheriff Haley dropped dead. One of the deputies ran up the road, but a bullet knocked him down, while the other two jumped for cover. Every one of the first six bullets had passed through Haley's body, for the warriors were all nursing a grudge; but when the other deputies took cover, Red Ryan leaped over the wall.

About all the pay they got in these ambushes and sudden assassinations were the guns of the men who had been killed, and Red snatched up Haley's rifle. Another man was in the act of stripping off Haley's pistols when he was burned across the rump by a bullet. Ryan sprang back behind the adobe wall and for an hour they shot back and forth at the clerk of the court and the deputy. Then they sneaked out the back way and that session of the court was over.

At O'Grady's store the fighting men gathered in bunches, other partisans took refuge in Sweeny's store. Warriors sought to pay off old grudges by shooting at any enemy they recognized, and most of the shots were answered; but, as night came on, the different parties congregated at the opposite ends of town. Mounted posses rode everywhere. They discovered each other at close range in the darkness and horses and men went down, but in the morning at daylight Red Ryan was called upon to surrender. His group of ten warriors was opposed by sixty fighting men, mostly fighting for pay; but, knowing what had happened to the other prisoners, he told them to turn their wolf loose.

The rifles began to pop from the windows of O'Grady's store, two buffalo-guns roared from the heights, and one defender went down; but in the middle of their shooting, lawyer Sweeny rode in with thirty-five Mexicans behind him. The Mexicans were three to one to the Americans on both sides, and were descended from Indian-fighting stock. They carried on the battle till dark, but on the morning of the second day the fighting began in earnest. Bullets smashed through Sweeny's wooden shutters, the sharpshooters killed another man, but with so many expert riflemen opposed to them, shooting through loopholes in the walls, lawyer Sweeny was holding them even.

He might have won the day, although he was far from being a warrior, when a woman broke through the lines and ran to Fort Stanton, nine miles away. She called on Colonel Dudley to stop this day-long madness, with women and children cooped up all over town and a hand-to-hand struggle imminent.

Dudley called out his men, two squadrons of Negro cavalry, and went down the road at a gallop. The bugles were sounding, two gatling guns rumbled to the front, when with sabres and carbines jingling they rode into the war-blasted town. It was a great triumph for the women, after the shooting of the last two days, and when the column halted in front of Sweeny's house even O'Grady's men came out. They mingled with the other warriors, the battle seemed to be over, but when Dudley ordered Sweeny to cease firing, saying nothing to the other side, two O'Grady men saw their chance.

Slipping down into the bed of Bonito Creek with cans of coal oil in their hands, they splashed them against the shattered doors and windows and waited to hear Sweeny's reply.

"This fight was started by O'Grady," answered the lawyer. "And as long as his men keep on shooting, my men will shoot back."

"You have heard my orders," responded Dudley; and marched his soldiers away. But hardly had Sweeny's warriors resumed their places in the house than they heard the crackle of flames. Black smoke flared up from the shattered back door and they caught the rank odor of kerosene. The house was afire and, when they rushed in to fight it, the enemy opened fire. Colonel Dudley had not ordered the O'Grady men to cease shooting. Since the affair appeared to be purely a civil conflict he could respond only to the request of the authorities.

Well, the sheriff was dead and all of his deputies were on O'Grady's pay roll. So no officer requested that Dudley intervene and the firing raged all day. When the defenders of Sweeny's house would have put the fire almost out, a savage attack from their enemies would allow it to start all over again. Room after room was abandoned until only the kitchen was left; and then, as darkness came on, the defenders made their break.

One wall had fallen down, exposing them to the fire of the men who gathered around. Three men were shot down before Sweeny appeared, and with a volley they mowed him down. Then six defenders rushed out together through the storm of bullets, leaped over the back wall and escaped. But Red Ryan had delayed to the end. He cocked both his pistols, waited a moment till the firing ceased, and dashed out, shooting his way. Every warrior was shooting wildly, intent upon getting his man, but Red shot right and left, never slackening his speed, until he leaped over the wall and was gone.

They counted their dead, then, and called for music — and a drink. Sweeny was dead. He had dared to oppose the Big Boss of Lincoln and the next day they laid him in his grave.

CHAPTER
TWENTY-ONE

The Shadow of the Big Boss

The sheriff was dead, Sweeny the lawyer was dead, and, for refusing to dance to the tune of their six-shooters, another lawyer passed out. From the expense of meeting his pay roll Major O'Grady went broke and died bankrupt. But the gay life of the outlaws went on. With the plains covered with mavericks and unbranded calves, and huge herds passing up the trail, it was no use working for wages as long as a man had a running-iron.

Martial law was declared and the outlaws left town, but Lincoln was a wreck. Governor Lew Wallace was sent west by President Hayes to straighten out the tangles of hate and he proclaimed a general amnesty. Then he, the Governor, drove down from Santa Fe and appealed to the outlaw, Red Ryan. Red had lived through it all and prospered. He saw no reason to change his ways. They would kill him, anyway, if they ever took him prisoner, and his enemies were still at large.

They were all at large and even the President of the United States could not make them cease fighting. Then Captain Jack Hightower, that maker of long trails, came back from a trip to Wyoming, and rode into Lincoln with one man. It was Pat Garrett, an old-time buffalo hunter, just elected sheriff, and he came to bring peace — and a sword.

Across the pommel of his saddle he still carried his old buffalo gun. It would shoot two miles, chambered a .45–90 cartridge and he had made a business of shooting buffalos for their hides until there were no more to shoot. The Indians still thought they had gone down a big hole, to emerge on the Judgment Day; but, having killed his share, Pat was open to any offer, even to taking on Ryan.

Red and his warriors had moved over to Three Rivers, where Butch Hardigan had a ranch and, with mavericks selling up to twenty dollars apiece, they never had far to go. When all other sources of income failed they could ride down and rob Henry Haught, and more than once Red had gazed upon Odette, and jerked his head and leered. There was no law of God or man that he would not break if he could, and her mother kept Odette inside the fort.

It was her instinct to drive all men away if they so much as looked at Odette. With her mass of smoky hair, her trim figure and bold violet eyes, she was the belle of all that country, even as she had charmed them on the Brazos. But she knew by the wicked look in his eyes that Red Ryan was positively dangerous and only one man dared stand up to him. Not Barney Hoops,

148

though he bristled like a dog when he sighted his enemy in the distance; but Ash Haught himself, ever ready for a fight. He drove them all away.

Hightower rode across the desert of sand and up the steep trail to where Beau McCutcheon was waiting. They had had the Lincoln County war since Captain Jack had ridden away; but when he came back from Wyoming all was changed. The Haughts had moved inside their adobe-built fort with its oakhewn door for a gate, but at sight of the Captain the Haughts shut the door, and Hightower and Garrett took the hint.

When they arrived at Johnson's spring, and the stone house on the hill, Hightower found the partners still there. For lack of more men Rye was ready to quit, but at sight of Pat Garrett he smiled.

"Our new sheriff," announced Hightower, shaking hands. "Here's a man that will do something, Rye."

Miles looked at Garrett, who stood six feet four in his socks, and decided that he would do.

"I've got a job for you," he said sarcastically. "Been saving it for a *man*. Butch Hardigan took a shot at me last week when he found me looking over his hides. On the slaughterhouse fence — half of them with Texas brands on them — and I decided I needed some help. Because my orders from the Captain were to take Red alive and —"

"I'll take him," promised Garrett.

"It can be done," admitted Miles. "But at the same time it's no child's play. Because Red Ryan and his gang make Butch's ranch their headquarters, and I reckon you've heard about Red."

"Mr. Garrett," observed Hightower, "has just been elected sheriff on account of Sheriff Haley's death, and his platform was 'Get Red Ryan!' But he'll need your assistance, both of you, till we get this mess straightened out. Martin Hockaday is responsible for starting all this trouble and now, when he might be of some help, he's busy fighting some lawsuit. A lawyer has plastered his whole ranch to satisfy a judgment he's got against him for fifty thousand dollars, but Martin swears he'll go to jail first and they're up in Las Vegas, fighting it out.

"We can't depend upon Mr. Hockaday for any moral support —" went on Hightower, "though he did have the grace to vote for Garrett — and the Cattlemen's Association is looking to me to bring these outlaws to book. The first man they want will be Butch Hardigan — we've got the warrant all ready to serve; and, after him —"

"Red Ryan," answered Garrett.

"We'll take 'em before Judge Bristol, over at Las Cruces; and Beau, I suppose you'll be on the jury. Be sure you do your duty."

"Yes, sir," responded McCutcheon, meekly.

"Of course," went on the Captain, "I know you'd rather get in on this fighting; but it is very important to keep that jury lined up. I blame Martin Hockaday more than anyone else for starting this Lincoln County War. He's made a joke of all this stealing and rustling until a jury would hardly convict. But this recent big killing has rather sobered them down, and perhaps they'll listen to me, now. This rustling must stop, and the way to stop it is —"

"Kill every son-of-a-goat that packs an iron," nodded Garrett.

"Well — maybe," assented Hightower. "I've got to be going now and you can use your own discretion. How's the cattle business progressing, Mr. McCutcheon? I've brought you a pair of glasses that may come in handy in watching that outlaw trail. It leads right down past Haught's fort, and I can see Haught has been losing cows. Sorry we can't have his help in breaking up this gang, but he's bitter against us all. If you want to sell some steers, arrange it with Sheriff Duran. I can't afford to appear in this sale at all or some one will claim I'm a cow-thief." He broiled a strip of beef, gnashed it savagely in front of the fire and rode off down the trail with a sigh.

It was a matter of regret with him that he had refused to buy Haught's steers, for it turned out he was an honest man; but twice before he had wanted to cut Hightower's herd, and that was something he would not stand. Hightower had even refused to buy steers from Hockaday when he found out that the herd was stolen, but he still regarded him as a friend, led astray by the spirit of the times. Everybody was stealing, it was the custom of the country; but this rustling would have to stop. Otherwise they would go out of business.

CHAPTER
TWENTY-TWO

The Scalp Hunter

All through this war Captain Hightower had kept on, bringing herd after herd from the Brazos, and the cattlemen at home had elected him President, though he was off on the trail half the time. But making money hand over fist, and carrying on the campaign to boot. In a land where an honest cowman was the noblest work of God, he had stood out for honesty to the end. It had cost him lots of money, but he did not regret it. And it showed that honesty paid.

While the poor white trash and nesters were stealing a few cows he was selling a thousand, every one marked with his road-brand, and coming back for more. But until he came upon Pat Garrett he thought Red Ryan had won. Pat and Red had worked side by side in the old days and regarded each other as friends. Each man was a killer, as cold as a stone, but the cards said Garrett would win. He had the law behind him, had lived a hard life, and in every way he was *hard*. And when Ryan heard what Pat's platform had been he promised to kill him *first*.

"Well, boys," observed Garrett, as Hightower rode away, "you've been having it pretty soft, I can see that.

Branding up these mavericks, putting in windows and doors, rocking up your spring and all that. But if you're going to ride with me —"

"I'll ride with you," answered Miles, defiantly.

"We will start an hour before dawn," said Pat, and curled up before the fireplace like a dog. His legs were so long they almost touched the ground when he stepped up on his black mule, and he had had to make leggings out of buffalo-hide to reach the tops of his boots. There was something wry and cynical about his twisted smile and he went after Red like a wolfer when the cattlemen offered a big reward. He would have to kill Ryan in order to get his scalp, but killing was his business.

As if awakened by some hidden mechanism he roused up an hour before dawn. There was frost in the air, but he did not wear a coat. Just a fringed buckskin shirt with half the strings gone where he had cut them off for whangs. He set off without looking back or even waiting for breakfast and when he saw Miles behind him he seemed genuinely surprised. But he did not say a word until he came to where the trail split.

"Know anything about this country?" he asked, and Rye Miles grunted assent.

"Been all over it," he said.

"What's the best way to get to that slaughterhouse?" inquired Pat, and Rye jerked his head to the left.

With his saddle-gun under his knee and two pistols in his belt he watched the ridges like a hawk, but Garrett still clung to his old Sharp's rifle, balanced across the horn of his saddle. By simply pointing it

153

from where it lay and pulling the trigger he could beat any man shooting at close range; and up to two miles — when he got a stand on the buffalos — he figured on a bull for every cartridge.

The sun was just up when they reached the post slaughterhouse and hid out to watch for Hardigan. He rode in, just as horse-faced as ever, driving a small band of cattle before him, and Garrett moved the muzzle of his gun. Hardigan saw it and reached for his pistol, but when he saw the twisted smile behind the gun he stopped and held up his hands.

"Unbuckle your belt," said Garrett, "and put your guns on the ground. This is Mr. Hardigan, I believe?"

"'Hardigan!'" repeated the butcher, unbuckling his gun-belt but neglecting to put it down. "Oh, you mean the butcher? He'll be along in a minute — with some of the byes, you know. I'm just the hired man that does the butchering."

"Ye-es!" mocked Rye Miles, rising up from behind a rock; and Hardigan hesitated — for a second. Then he dropped his pistols to the ground and looked behind him anxiously.

"The byes will be along anny minute," he observed, speaking to Garrett. "You're familiar with them all, of carse. There's Red Ryan and Charley Bowdre, Tom O'Phaillard and all the rest of them —"

"Then I'll wait," said Pat Garrett, and laughed. "Are those your steers, Mr. Hardigan?"

"These? Mine?" Butch's red eyes were big with wonderment.

"Or are these your hides?" inquired the sheriff.

154

"They are!" answered Miles, "and I'll take my oath I saw Hardigan hang them on the fence. This is the same man that took a shot at me, Mr. Garrett, when he caught me reading the brands."

"Oh, is this Misther Garrett, our new sheriff?" exclaimed Hardigan with a winning smile; but Garrett picked up Hardigan's pistols without even answering him and beckoned him down the trail.

Judge Bristol was waiting in the courtroom at Mesilla for the prisoner to be brought in and, after Miles had identified him and given his evidence, the Judge ordered Butch locked up. Then, as the wheels of justice began to turn, he sentenced him to two years. Just to get him out of the way. Beau McCutcheon was on the jury, with eleven other good men and true and while they were going through the routine of sending Butch to prison, Pat Garrett headed back to Butch's ranch. But Red Ryan was gone, and tall Tom Pickett, Charley Bowdre and all the rest. They had left in a day and there was snow on the ground before they were even heard of.

They rode into White Oaks to get a drink and, on the way out, Red shot at a deputy sheriff in what he considered a friendly way. But a posse of officers rode after them, they were surprised at Coyote Springs and Ryan was lucky to escape on foot, after having his horse shot out from under him. White Oaks was an old, deserted mining camp, where the outlaws had spent thousands of dollars for the drinks, but the tide was turning against them, and once more they dropped from sight. They were doing a big business in stealing Texas cattle and selling them in southern New Mexico, picking up as many more on the way back and driving them to northern Texas. But Texas was the loser at both ends of the line and Garrett spread his nets for Red. The country was large, most of the Mexicans were his friends and they kept him fully informed; but the news got out that Ryan was coming to Fort Sumner to celebrate Christmas Eve.

There was dancing and drinking and Tom and Jerry, but someone had told Garrett the way they would go out and he rode in with fifteen men. Fighting men, too; but not outlaws, not cow-thieves. They were gunmen, killers, but they fought within the law, though as yet with very little principle. It was just that the war had roused men at last to the danger of all this stealing. Hundreds of thousands of settlers were moving into the West, but they all went by beautiful Lincoln and the millions of acres around Deep Lake. The country had got a bad name and half the stores in Lincoln were deserted. But Pat Garrett was still trying to fulfill his election promise and get Red Ryan or bust. He entered Fort Sumner after dark and took refuge in the old military hospital. It was vacant and abandoned now — all the better for Pat — and while scouts watched the road the posse played poker by the fire.

Midnight came, with its yelling and shooting; and then; out from town, five horsemen came at a gallop. No one knew who they were, but Red Ryan was in town so the posse stepped out into the moonlight, Pat Garrett with his big buffalo-gun.

"Throw up your hands," he said on general principles; but still the outlaws came on. A man out in front reached down for his six-shooter, the buffalo-gun went off and shot him above the heart. The rest stopped short, realized that they had run into an ambush, whirled around and clattered away. Then the posse closed around Tom O'Phaillard, Red Ryan's right-hand man, and watched him die in agony. But Red Ryan was not there.

CHAPTER
TWENTY-THREE

Stinking Springs

Still the wolf pack was getting closer, Garrett had got his first man and driven Ryan pell-mell into the hills. A rancher came in and reported him heading north, towards an old, abandoned house called Stinking Springs. There was a blizzard blowing, the ground was covered with snow which had covered up the tracks, but at midnight Pat Garrett set out again, to kill Red Ryan or die.

At daylight, with three picked men, he crept up behind the cutbank of the wash and looked over the top at the door, not thirty feet away. They were there, for two horses were standing outside waiting hopelessly for their riders to awake, and Garrett hid his horses out of range. Then he settled down in the whirling storm and at last a man came out.

It was Charlie Bowdre, bringing out a *morral* of corn for his horse, and the old buffalo-gun came up.

"Throw up your hands!" ordered Garrett; but Bowdre reached for his gun.

Bang! went the rifle and Bowdre staggered.

Bang Bang! And he almost went down. But he turned and stumbled back through the doorway, and they could hear every word that was said.

"They've got you, Charlie," said Ryan. "Plumb through the chest — you can't live. See if you can get one of them before you die!"

He shoved him out into the stillness and Garrett let him come on. It was only thirty feet and Bowdre had nearly got to the ditch before he pitched forward and died.

"Come out of that, you fellows!" ordered Garrett; but Ryan was not a man to quit. He was safe, behind the stone walls, and he had his horse inside, a racing mare he was fond of. But these were different men from the ones he had encountered when he was shooting up the town at Lincoln. With rifle bullets they cut the ropes of the tied horses and killed another mount, blocking the doorway.

"Better come out," advised Pat; but he could hear them trying to dig loopholes through the walls. So he let them dig on in the cold.

"What's the use?" inquired a voice at last. "He's killed two men and he'll kill all the rest of us. We might as well give up."

"Not me!" cursed Ryan and the besiegers lit a fire to boil a pot of coffee. Down out of the wind they had coffee and bacon and eggs, while the outlaws were hungry and cold. It was more than human nature could stand and, as sundown approached they showed a white handkerchief on a stick.

"We'll come out," said Ryan, "before we freeze to death, if you'll promise not to shoot. That coffee smell is too much for us."

"Hands up!" commanded Garrett, and Red Ryan came out first.

He crawled out humbly, over the body of the dead horse which had blocked his last chance to escape; and the posse put the handcuffs on every one of them before they gave them a drink. Then they mounted them on the slowest horses they had and tied their feet together under the ponies' bellies.

It was a long way to Mesilla, the old courthouse near Las Cruces where Judge Bristol awaited their coming, and there they were put in leg-irons. Garrett was taking no chances with these men he knew were just waiting to kill him. Bristol had refused, once before, to hold court in Lincoln; but this was in Doña Ana County, where Manuel Duran de Chaves held forth.

The wheels of justice were grinding slowly, but they would grind exceedingly fine. There was something in the look of this grim man on the bench which warned Ryan he could expect no mercy.

Duran was still the same old Manuel — courteous, kindly, efficient — but Beau knew he had not wholly forgotten when Red Ryan had been there before. Then he had jumped the Comanches in the midst of their trading and killed three of them before they could escape. Then returned to the river, rounded up every steer with a Texas brand on it and driven them all away. It had been a great loss to the Mexican population, especially to the comancheros, but Duran had shaken his head when they begged him to interfere. They had let Hockaday take the steers and, inside of a week, every animal had been stolen again. By this same Ryan

160

who now stood before the judge and answered him with downcast eyes.

He had been the spear and front of the Texas invasion which, crossing the barren Staked Plains, had brought the first steers to Horsehead Crossing and driven them up the Pecos. They had fought off the Apaches and Comanches, riding roughshod over the Mexicans, even robbing the man for whom they worked; and at the end of it all Red stood at the bar of justice, charged with murder and with no one to defend him.

"Have you a lawyer?" inquired the judge, and Ryan shook his head.

He had stolen thousands of cattle and sold them to beef buyers and butchers, but no man would defend him now.

"Have you no money to engage an attorney?" asked the judge, and once more Ryan hung his head. While he had been riding in the lead of his gang, giving mavericks to ranchers, feeding the Mexicans with yearlings, he had been the outlaw king of New Mexico. But, with all the easy money that went through his hands he had never saved a dime.

"Then if you wish," went on the judge, imperturbably, "I will appoint a man to defend you."

It had come to that, then. He had had to take the pauper's oath and the prosecuting attorney sat smiling. Someone had killed the previous prosecuting attorney when he was going to open court, but here was another one — smiling. They had killed all the lawyers in Lincoln — and killed the sheriff, too. But after the

161

shooting was all over, Red Ryan stood before the bench. A deputy United States Marshal and a deputy sheriff stood guard to prevent his escape; and, conveniently near, Pat Garrett, his old friend, with his terrifying buffalo-gun.

Pat had been elected with the slogan: "Get Red Ryan." And, while he was getting Red, he had picked up three other men who had defied the law for years. Yet Garrett had got them all, and in the jury box sat another man Red knew. Beau McCutcheon, who had put his back against the heavy timbers at Fort Davis and let him out of the snake-hole; Bloody Head, who had led the battle against the Comanches, yet refused to cut another man's herd. He sat impassively when man after man testified that he, Ryan, had murdered Sheriff Haley. Shot him in the back from behind and robbed him of his fine rifle.

After that the appeals of the attorney for the defense sounded rather weak and inane. The jury retired and cast but one vote before the bailiff brought them in.

The clerk of the court read the verdict forthwith, to the effect that the defendant was guilty of murder and they fixed his punishment at death.

It was then that, for the first time, Red sensed the giant conspiracy to railroad him to certain death; but he stood up boldly while the judge passed sentence — the same judge he had promised to kill. On the 13th of May he would be hanged by the neck until he was dead, dead, dead.

Well, that was what he had expected; but when two death guards took him back to his cell it came as an unpleasant surprise. Both were personal enemies of his, and they put the handcuffs on very tight. Then they clamped the shackles on his legs and fitted them — a little tight.

"Aha!" said Bob Ollinger, the deputy United States Marshal whose partner Ryan had killed. "You'll get what's coming to you now. My old friend Bob Beckwith will be waiting to see you when you step off and go to hell."

He was a rough-looking man who wore his hair long and dressed in buckskin like a plainsman. Three notches were cut on the handle of his six-shooter and his eyes were of the pale steel-blue that is supposed to be the mark of a killer. It was for just this reason that Garrett had appointed him head of the death watch. Ollinger hated Red and was forever seeking to tempt him to escape, so he could shoot him in the back. The other guard was different, though with just as good reason for killing Ryan, if he could. For, not two months before, Red had slain Deputy Sheriff Carlyle, when he was making a dash to escape. With any reason at all, Bell would have put a bullet through him; but as Ollinger rode Ryan day and night, his partner on the death watch soon got tired of it.

"Leave the kid alone," he said to Ollinger. "Within a month he'll be dead, and that's good enough for me. He murdered Jim Carlyle and I'd shoot him for a nickel, but as long as he's quiet and leaves us alone, don't bother him all the time."

They loaded him into a hack and took him over the mountains to the place where he was sentenced to die, but the jail at Lincoln would hardly hold a drunk and

163

Garrett moved him into the courtroom. It was a large airy place on the second floor of O'Grady's old store, well away from any chance to rescue him and at the same time absolutely safe. With the handcuffs on his wrists day and night and a heavy pair of leg-irons on his ankles, he was as safe as he could be kept. There wasn't a real prison in New Mexico.

The arrest of this one man and his sentence to death had broken up his whole gang. There was no one who dared come to his rescue, though Red Ryan might have done it for them. But the fear of Pat Garrett had cast a shadow over the whole community and Pat was determined that Ryan should hang. Every night for a month he tried the handcuffs and leg-irons, he slept in the same room and watched him close; but the time came at last when he had to go to White Oaks to order the timbers for the scaffold.

No one had been hanged in Lincoln County in the regular, accepted way. They might have been strung up to a tree somewhere or suspended from the end of a wagon-tongue, but Garrett felt the need of a gallows to carry out the order of the court. Three weeks before the fatal Friday, the 13th, he rode down to White Oaks to make the final arrangements, and before he went he climbed the crooked stairs to see that his prisoner was safe.

Red Ryan was sitting across the table from Bell, who was playing him Mexican monte.

"Well, boys," said Pat, "got to go out of town on a little official business. Good morning, Red — is he perfectly safe?"

164

"If it's that gallows you're thinking about," spoke up Ollinger, "you can't git back too soon. I'm counting the hours until I can see Red Ryan, dancing a jig on thin air. It's just three weeks until I spring the trap and —"

"He's perfectly safe," stated Bell.

"Handcuffs and shackles all right?"

"They're fitted so tight he's worked all the skin off and —"

"Maybe he's trying to get loose in the night?"

"It can't be done," laughed Red. "Or I'd've skipped out, long ago. No. Go ahead and get your scaffold built and let's have it over with before Ollinger talks himself to death. All he thinks about, day and night, is how pretty I'll look when I'm dancing a jig in hell."

"Well, I'm sorry for you, Red," said Garrett, "but it's got to be done. And Bell and Bob, I'm depending on you not to go to sleep at the switch. Watch him every minute — don't get too near him — and look out he don't grab your guns. I'm depending on you, now. So long."

He nodded his head at Red and beckoned Ollinger down the hall-way that led to the flight of steps.

"Everything all right?" he asked.

"No!" answered Ollinger. "Bell is reading him the paper, and first thing we know Red will grab him. He's a slick little feller, always up to some trick —"

"Stick around, then," advised Garrett. "Red has got to do something, to keep his mind off of being hung. Let Bell read the paper and play monte with him, but keep your eagle eye out till I get back."

165

"Don't worry, Pat," said Ollinger, "we'll watch him like a goat. How's this for keeping him scared up?"

He stepped to a closet where their guns were kept and came out with a double-barreled shotgun.

"See this?" he asked of Red. "There's eighteen buckshot in each barrel, and I reckon a man who gets them will feel it."

"Yes," smiled Ryan. "You may get one yourself." And he went on playing cards.

CHAPTER
TWENTY-FOUR

The Escape

That was the way Red took it, with a joke and a smile, but he was fighting the handcuffs all night. He was starving himself, and they thought he had lost his appetite, with the hanging only a few days off. But, right when Garrett was gone and there was a chance to make a break, Charlie Wall killed four Mexicans at Tularosa and came to Lincoln to escape being mobbed.

The scene of the killing was in Doña Ana County, and he was afraid of Manuel Duran; but Pat Garrett was an old friend of his and Pat let him stay in the courtroom. Stay and wear his pistols and sleep there at night, and he had four Mexicans with him who were around under foot, day and night. And the time was getting short. Red wanted to be alone — with Bell.

About five o'clock that evening Bob Ollinger took Charlie Wall and the four armed prisoners to the hotel across the street for supper, and at last Red Ryan was alone. Bell sat in a chair several paces away, reading the newspaper, as was his custom, although Ollinger had warned him against it. Because a man with his eyes on the paper could not watch as active a prisoner as Ryan.

167

The time had come, but Red did not hurry. He had learned to slip his left hand free, no matter how tightly they clamped it and, timing his leap until Bell raised the paper up, he made a spring, striking him over the head with the steel cuff. Bell threw up both hands to protect his head and Red got what he was after. The Gun. He grabbed it out of its scabbard and shot Bell with his own pistol as he ran.

Bell got to the head of the stairway before he tumbled and fell dead, fetching up on Geiss, the jailer, who was sitting at the foot of the stairs. Of course Geiss stampeded, rushing out the gate towards the hotel and Ollinger came on the run.

"Bell has killed Red," Geiss shouted, and Ollinger slackened his pace to a walk. This was what he had expected — Bell had only beaten him to it — and there was no hurry whatever, now. But as he walked across the street Red stuck his head out the window, with Bob's shotgun in his hand. Feeling the body of Bell fall upon him Geiss had thought it was Red. But, instead of being killed, Red had smashed in the door of the closet where all their arms were kept and snatched out Ollinger's gun.

"Hello, Bob!" he called in honeyed tones; and put eighteen buckshot through his heart. That was what Bob had promised *him*.

After that Red hobbled back to the armory, buckled two belts of cartridges around his waist, and two Colt's pistols. Then, taking a Winchester rifle in his hand, he walked in his shackles to pick up the shotgun, and stepped out on the front porch.

"Take that," he said, emptying the shotgun into Ollinger's body and all the people in the hotel rushed out. But not to kill Red, not for shooting the deputy United States Marshal. Charlie Wall and his Mexicans were all armed, but they wanted to see Red get away. He had to procure a file before he could cut himself loose from the leg-irons, but he still had time to dance a jig before he mounted and rode away.

The black pony he clambered up on, encumbered with his guns and ammunition, put his head down and bucked him off, but he handed his rifle to the jailer to hold — and the jailer gave it back. Then Ryan galloped off to the west, looking back and giving three cheers.

When Garrett heard the news on the streets of White Oaks he hired every man in the county who would fight to cut off Red at the Line.

"Mexico!" he cursed. "That's where he'll go, and the Mexicans will make him their king. I knowed all the time that scaffold would be my Jonah. We ain't educated up to it yet."

Pat Garrett was chagrined at the way the courts of law had marred his plans to get Red. In a country without a decent jail in it the Judge had set the day for the hanging almost two months ahead and, before the scaffold could be laboriously constructed, Red Ryan was far away. On the way out of town he stopped at a Mexican ranch and filled up with coffee and beans. Then he went to another ranch where the man was a blacksmith and got him to strike off his irons. After that he disappeared and, while Garrett raked New Mexico for him, he kept out of sight for months.

Captain Hightower had stock detectives all over the country, collecting the cattle stolen from his ranches and driving them back to the home range, but he turned them all loose and put his men on the trail. Only now their orders were different. After this last failure of the law, the formality of a hanging would be dispensed with. If they ever came within range of this prince of outlaws he would be shot on sight, and no questions asked. But now Red Ryan was gone.

He was gone, but not forgotten, and soon the Mexicans began to sing songs about him and the good deeds he had done. Robbing the rich to feed the poor. Always the friend of the Mexicans. But while Captain Hightower was searching for Ryan he found Martin Hockaday — in jail. He had been there for months, while all the fighting was going on, and his vast empire had fallen in ruins. A lawyer had taken over the old claims against him and, when he resolutely refused to pay them, had thrown him into the Las Vegas jail. But, having been robbed once, Hockaday had lost all faith in lawyers. A good attorney could have had him released in twenty-four hours; Captain Hightower got the claims reduced; but Hockaday swore an oath that, while they might collect from his heirs, they would never collect from him.

It is the law in New Mexico, passed down from old Spanish days, that a man can be imprisoned for debt. Another lawyer raked up other claims, he piled Pelion on Ossa in order to break Hockaday's proud spirit; and so, while his cattle were being stolen by the thousand, Martin Hockaday lay in jail. His Salamander safe had been stuffed to the doors with quit-claim deeds for land; millions of acres on both sides of the Pecos, giving him absolute control of the water. And when the man whom he had trusted to handle his affairs took advantage of his absence to abscond, even then he would not pay. And meanwhile some sixty thousand head of cattle were running wild on the open plains.

Captain Hightower came riding in at last from his great ranch in the Panhandle of Texas. He had sent out fifteen of the best stock detectives in the country, but things were growing worse. Even the law, which he had always sworn by, had turned out a dismal failure and Garrett was ready to resign. There was no law to be enforced as long as the jails would not hold; and, with Red Ryan still loose, even across the Rio Grande in Mexico, that one man could thwart them all.

He was a devil in human form — a gay, laughing devil — and now he could not be found. Some said he was hiding so close that he could hear every word they said. He still drank at the bars in half the saloons in New Mexico, and yet Pat Garrett could not find him.

Garrett sent two good men across the border into Old Mexico and they came back without seeing a sign. No, he was not there, this man they had once taken and let slip through their hands. And all on account of the law's delays when a six-shooter would have done just as well as a scaffold. Captain Hightower saw them all, even Beau McCutcheon on the hill, and implored them to use their eyes. Red was there. He was there somewhere, and the Mexicans knew it. But they laughed, they shrugged their shoulders, they would not tell.

Twenty stock detectives were in hiding, besides the fifteen at work, the cattle were being driven off — two ways. And could no man find out what any kid might tell him; or any sweetheart, if she would? Well, it was there before their eyes if they would only look around; and the next time Red Ryan came under their guns — or were the Mexicans too smart for them?

He departed, still muttering in his beard, and it was left to Manuel Duran de Chaves to find out what everybody knew.

CHAPTER
TWENTY-FIVE

Enough

Don Manuel had seen many people come and go since he had settled down on the Rio Grande. Apaches, Navajos, Comanches, Utes; and Mexicans and Texans, too. They all had their ways and Duran had learned to know them, for on the river his word was law. When the Apaches went on the warpath they kept away from Las Cruces and Mesilla; and in fifteen years he had not killed a man, so well was he respected and feared. Even the Texans feared him, though he was always so polite; but there was one man among them he could trust.

The red-headed little Beau who lived at Johnson's Canyon and always fed the Indians when they passed. Or anybody else — he knew when people were hungry and always had a beef hung up. Duran knew he could trust him not to tell all he heard, and this Ryan was getting rough. The women were afraid of him — and the men-folks, too — but Bloody Head was always polite. Even with the *pelado* Mexicans. And he had a girl, himself.

Such a pretty little girl — he watched her through his glasses and smiled when she went out to ride — but he never went down to call. The Haught men had warned him off — the best boy of them all — and he did not wish to kill her brother, Ash. They were hard men to handle, quick to take offense, treating their Mexican servants like slaves; but if Seraphin Ortega, the adobe-maker, was sure Beau could be trusted he would tell him something, maybe.

The Haughts were still making bricks, still building up the walls of their fort, still keeping their women inside; but there was something Seraphin knew. He had built his own house away from the rest, but his women were afraid of one man. Red rode down at night from Three Rivers Canyon, to see a woman who was there. Not Seraphin's daughter — he kept her too close — but there is always such a woman. And such a man.

He came at night, when the Haughts had gone to bed, but the women all knew who he was. The same man the Texans were hunting for, though they did not guess he was there. He came and went boldly, and he paid his woman in gold from some cache that he had in the hills, but it was some other woman he sought. The same proud woman he had tried to steal once before when she had slapped him in the face and run. Her brother, the next day, had tried to whip this man and Colorado had rapped him over the head. Yes, it was the same man — Red — but how to put the Texans on his trail!

Duran visited them often — they were all Las Cruces Mexicans — and at last one man told him the news. It was no secret among the women; but Seraphin, the adobe-maker, knew. With a reward on his head, with forty men hunting for him, Red had come back to his hiding-place at Three Rivers, just over the hills from Lincoln. Seraphin knew, for he had a dog that growled and a daughter that needed to be watched. Red came by the door one night and Seraphin looked out and saw him try the Haught gate. But it was the women who found out what he sought. It was Odette.

The fine, tall woman with the smoke-colored hair who felt herself so much above the rest. The one who rode out boldly, with only her brother, Ash, and he a man easily killed. Red had asked his *querida* if she could not lure Ash away, and she had guessed the rest. Red was going south, to the land of mañana, where a man need not of necessity get married, and he wanted this woman to take with him. She hated him now, and feared him, but he had set his heart on Odette. There were other men, of course, who wanted to marry her and would give a horse for her smile. They were big, they were strong; but the Ranger Miles had taken her fancy, though Barney Hoops had warned him away. But when she saw him riding by she showed herself in the gateway, and the women could guess the rest.

Much more they guessed, while they were washing their clothes and grinding *tortillas* by the fire; but they did not think it necessary to tell their husbands, for men do not always understand. Still there was one man among them who knew what was going on, since he had a young daughter who needed watching and who had caught Red's roving eye. Red dropped in in passing, to visit with her father and inquire about the making of the walls; and once he had asked idly about the Mescalero Apaches and how, by sawing with a rough rawhide *reata,* they could cut through the adobes like paper.

Idle talk, of course, but at the end of the evening, he had asked where Odette lived. Odette and all the others, but Seraphin was not born yesterday. He had served as a soldier with Manuel Duran de Chaves and had the courage to tell all he knew. Not the first time either and, after thanking him for his confidence and finding out just how the ground lay, Duran had given him the rest of the bottle.

Here was something which Don Manuel had suspected, for he was the *patron* of all that country and esteemed it to be his first duty to look after the interests of his people. He had got Seraphin Ortega the job to move out with his *gente* and build this fort for the Haughts; and, while they were working, they made houses for themselves, down on the edge of the wash. The men made the bricks, mixing the mud day by day and laying the adobes out to dry, and Colonel Haught had been well pleased with the result. His fort had been made quickly, to keep out evil men, and in the end they had built the gateway, exactly like the one at Cebolleta, which their fathers had built before them.

Those walls had been made of stone, four feet wide and ten feet high, with every room on the inside, where they could stand on the roof and fight over the top. They were built continuously, of plain adobe bricks, and the entrance was closed by a narrow gate, formed of planks two feet thick which were fastened by a heavy iron bar. Five thousand Navajos had hurled themselves against the walls but Cebolleta had never been taken and Haught had built a fort just like it. But when this Red Ryan planned to saw his way through and steal the Señora's daughter, that was something that called for action.

Duran had engaged the men to build the fort and the Colonel had paid him promptly. He was a hard man and a stern one but he did not steal their cattle, like the Texans from over on the Pecos. Nor did his men fight among themselves all the time, like the warriors of Lincoln. They were a clan, like the *gentes* of the Mexicans, who honored the word of their *patron*, and if Red had his way their fort would lay in ruins, like the buildings in old Lincoln. And Garrett had married a woman of Las Cruces, so in a way he was a Mexican himself. Not a straight Texan, like Haught, with his overbearing ways, treating his workmen like dogs. But still he was honest. He paid.

So with many things to consider for the safety of his people Don Manuel decided to act. But first he must find a Texan he could trust — and who else but Beau McCutcheon? He was kind, he was honest, and he fed the Indians beef. That showed his heart was good.

Two days later, when his trip to Three Rivers would be forgotten, Duran rode up the old Jornada de Muerto, where a traveler had gone so long without eating or drinking that he looked like a shrunken dead man.

"Good morning, Don Beau," greeted Buran. "How is your health, my friend? I was wondering where I could get some more steers, in place of those which were stolen by the Comanches, first, and then sold to the *comancheros*, and then stolen back by Don Martin Hockaday. Then stolen all over again by your friend Red Ryan —"

"He is no friend of mine," broke in Beau.

"No?" said Duran. "Then perhaps we can talk business; after I have bought, perhaps, some of your steers. They are big and fat, from standing around the water-hole and feeding out on the plains. I can give you ten dollars a head, or maybe fifteen, or twenty."

"You can have all you want for ten," smiled Beau, "and I will help you drive them home. Then some more wild cattle will come down from the mountains and I will have as many more. I have not forgotten, Don Manuel, that it was you who guided me to this spot."

"I made a good neighbor, and a good friend," replied Duran. "But you are right. Some others will come. So we will round up these mavericks and take them to Las Cruces. And on the way, when no one can overhear us, I will speak of something else. I wonder if you have noticed, my friend, that your camp is being watched — from that hill."

"Yes indeed," laughed McCutcheon. "He is a fugitive from justice who is hiding from Pat Garrett and his men. But I leave him a little beef and he hides on that hill when he sees the sheriff coming in."

"To be sure," agreed Duran. "And a man must eat. But this man, as I know, is no friend of yours. He searches your house when you are gone."

"I have seen his tracks," answered Beau soberly. "But never have I seen his face. He wears moccasins, but he is not an Apache."

178

"He is a spy," exclaimed Duran, hotly. "Sent from Haught's fort to watch your every move. Perhaps he is waiting to kill you."

"No," replied McCutcheon. "But you know the Haught outfit — they think every man is a thief. I reckon he is watching, to catch me killing a calf, and then he will have me arrested."

"If you placed a bullet near him," suggested Manuel, "he would go away and not come back. But there are two other men who take to the hills when they see me, and you of course know best. Even the ravens know your camp and fly down to get meat, but ravens can be your friends. When they see a man coming they fly down and croak. That may keep you from being killed."

"It is part of my job," said Beau, "to stay here and see who goes by. I am paid one hundred dollars by my friend, Captain Hightower, to report to him, every month."

"There is a man I did not like at first," confessed Duran, as they rode along the trail. "But since he has brought in these stock detectives and ordered them to respect every brand, I have had to change my mind. But what of this new sheriff he has got elected? Do you like Pat Garrett? Do you trust him?"

"He is working for my *patron*," said McCutcheon, "and that is enough for me. What is it you have in mind?"

"The Mexicans are all laughing at him, because his prisoner escaped, but Red Ryan is a desperate man. Would you, who are so brave, dare to meet him? But no, I do not say that. Have you one or two friends you can trust, to kill, if necessary, this man?"

"I have," replied Beau, "if I get what you mean. We Texans stand together."

"Then go to the fort of Colonel Haught," said Duran. "Go with your gun in your hand, and take your two Texas friends. I do not like these Texans, if the truth must be told, but even they have their use. Now listen to what I say. A man is to be killed, and you Texans can do it, but no one must ever know. I pass the word to you, and you tell your friends; but me, I know nothing about it.

"You know my people, and how with them no secret is safe. Yet there is one secret — the greatest of all — which the Texans can never guess, though half the Mexicans know. Red Ryan has come back to Three Rivers Canyon, he is hiding in the mountains, and all the Mexican women know. He comes down at night, when the dogs have ceased barking, and goes to one woman, outside the fort. She lives in the last house, on the edge of the wash. I hope you can get him there. But if all our plans fail go to the first house in the row and inquire for Seraphin. Enough. Have I talked too much?"

"Not with me," answered Beau. "I am your friend."

"Then do not go near the place for one week. And carry your gun in your hand."

CHAPTER
TWENTY-SIX

Two Friends

A week was not too much to find Garrett and Miles, and even then Pat would not believe.

"Here?" he scoffed. "Right over the mountain from Lincoln, with a big reward on his head? Red Ryan is in Mexico and I know it. But all right, I'll try anything. The Mexicans all know something, I see that."

"He comes in late," went on McCutcheon. "When the dogs have settled down for the night. In the last house — down the gulch — and if I'd tell you the rest you'd believe me. He's got his eye on a woman."

"What woman?" demanded Miles, standing up.

"Never mind," answered Beau. "Just be there."

"I've been hearing the same thing for a month," grumbled Garrett, "but we might meet him in the road. Or going out."

"Or we might meet him coming in," said Rye. "Come on. What are we waiting for? Right now!"

"Now it is!" repeated Garrett, despondently. "If we get him at all it will be by some play like this, when we change our minds and turn back."

They rode in early, tying their horses up the gulch and carrying their boots as they walked down to the last house, but the place was silent as the grave. They stood in complete darkness, looking up over the cut bank, listening to the noises of the night. There was a light in the next house, a smell of bacon frying, and then a man came out.

"That's him!" whispered Garrett. "Look out!"

They stood there waiting; dark figures came and went, and then all was silent again.

"He got away from us," mumbled Pat. "But I'd know that stoop anywhere. Come on, let's go up to the house."

He led the way then up a plank walk, newly made, with cottonwood trees set in regular rows, and as the door swung open and Seraphin peeped out Garrett motioned his friends to wait. There was a murmur of Spanish inside, the squeak of a bed as Pat sat down on the edge. Then the sound of footsteps as some one came running, barefoot, along the planks. Some Mexican kid, they thought. A feeling of apathy had come over them, after their long hours of waiting in the dark, and they did not even get up. Miles had got his spur caught beneath the plank walk and it rattled as he jerked it loose.

"*Quien es?*" asked a voice. "Who is it?"

"Don't be scared," responded Beau, out of the darkness; and the Mexican started back and drew his pistol.

"Who is it?" he demanded again.

"*No ley asi* — it makes no difference," replied Miles, seeing a butcher knife in his hand. "Go ahead and get your meat."

182

It hung there against the side of the house, what was left of a shoulder of beef, and the boy reached up to cut a slice. Then he leaped back, pointing his pistol, and demanded again, querulously:

"Who is it? What do you want?"

Again the old apathy, coming from nerves let down, settled over them and they did no reply. What was it to them if the Mexican got his meat? Or was scared when he discovered two men? In the dark Red Ryan looked meager and small and his back had a decided stoop, like a boy who had worked too hard. For a moment he stood with his pistol drawn, pointing straight at McCutcheon's breast. Then he backed in the open door, still carrying his butcher knife, and at the sound of his voice Beau jumped up.

"Who are they?" it asked, and in the black darkness Garrett recognized his man. But in sitting down on the edge of the bed he had caught his long holster under him, and he did not dare to move. Red stood so close he could reach out and touch him. He knew his voice when he spoke to Beau. But inside the house Red could barely make out Seraphin as he lay stretched out on the bed.

"That's him," whispered Ortega. And Pat Garrett grabbed for his gun.

"Who's that?" cried Ryan, backing up, and for the first time he stepped into the moonlight.

Garrett raised his pistol and shot twice, plunging out as he did so and stooping low. Behind him came Seraphin Ortega, scared as if he had seen a ghost. They stood there, guns in hand, not daring to speak, hardly

183

knowing what was going on. Then, from inside, they heard the gurgle of blood and Garrett put up his gun. "I got him, boys," he said. "That was Red."

CHAPTER
TWENTY-SEVEN

Colonel Haught Again

Even in death they were frightened of this man whom they had taken for a Mexican kid. They lit a candle at last and thrust it in through the window and there lay Red Ryan, dead. He had been shot through the heart, and lay sprawling, his gun still grasped in his hand.

Now the women came running, they set up a wail and Garrett drew his men outside.

"Out of here," he ordered, as the women began to weep; and they rode back to camp the same night. Other men galloped by them, they were spreading the news everywhere like the warnings of an Indian uprising. At last it was out. Ryan had come to his death by the hand of Pat Garrett, who had set out to get him from the first. Pat had been the only man to know what was going on when he heard Red's voice outside. And even in the dark he shot straight.

They rode home in silence, looking back across the White Sands to where at dawn they saw people swarming in. From Ruidoso, from Lincoln, from

Tularosa, from every place where the word had spread, and at last Pat Garrett spoke up.

"Well, boys," he said, "here's how it happened. We were looking for someone else and we turned back to Three Rivers to inquire. Then Red walked in on us — he was hiding all the time — and came down to get a chunk of meat. Nobody told us. It was all an accident. Isn't that right, Mr. McCutcheon? Because everybody will want to know."

"That's right," agreed Beau, and Miles grunted assent.

That was their story and they stuck to it for three days — until Captain Hightower came. He rode in down Three Rivers Canyon with eight stock detectives behind him, and they would have gone past without stopping if Colonel Haught had not come out of his fort. Many people had rushed in, asking insistent questions which he was unable to answer; and when he saw this man, the head and front of the whole movement, riding by without breaking his pace he stepped up on his horse and rode after him.

"Captain Hightower, sir!" he shouted, as his whole clan galloped out after him; and Hightower reined in his horse.

"Yes, sir," answered the Captain. "How do you do, Colonel Haught. And before you say another word I want to state that in no way do I hold this against you. Red Ryan is dead — and he died at Three Rivers — but you yourself I hold blameless."

"Blameless of what?" stormed Haught. "I hope, sir, that never for a moment did you think I was connected with his gang."

"Certainly not!" returned Hightowner, beginning to blink, "and I am glad at this time to say so. But there have been moments in the past —"

"When you treated me like a thief — and no gentleman!"

"Perhaps so," answered the Captain. "And if so, I apologize. We all make mistakes —"

"Mistakes!" yelled Haught. "When you rode by without stopping! Is that the way of a gentleman?"

"Perhaps not," admitted the Captain, turning red and beginning to shout. "But I have got something else to do besides talking over old mistakes. So if you will not accept my apology — which I never intended to make, anyway — you can go to hell, Mr. Haught!"

"Humph! The same to you, sir!" replied Haught, falling in with all his men behind him. "But now I've got you here I just want you to explain what you mean by hounding me with your stock detectives. I hardly parked my wagons when I came into this country and saw, in yonder gap of the mountain, the campfire of one of your spies. And ever since that day he has watched me through his glasses as if I were an ordinary thief."

"Well, I gave him those glasses, myself," said Hightower. "And you may be pleased to know that Mr. McCutcheon reports —"

"To hell with *him*!" burst forth Haught. "He broke jail when he came into this country and rode in on another man's horse."

187

"All the same," answered Hightower, "he is one of my men, and I will not hear a word against him. So if that is all you have to say I will bid you farewell, Mr. Haught."

"Farewell to you, then," scowled Haught. "But before I go I will mention one thing more. McCutcheon has built a fence at the mouth of his canyon, to keep all of my cows from his spring. He has branded every maverick and calf in his own iron, and only last week he sold forty-two grown steers to the sheriff of Doña Ana County. At ten dollars a head!"

"A very good buy," nodded Hightower. "Grown steers are selling at twenty. And, just to keep people like you from making their dirty insinuations, I refused to buy McCutcheon's steers at any price. But he had his orders from the Cattlemen's Association to brand any maverick he could ketch."

"And you gave that order, sir?"

"I gave that order," acknowledged the Captain.

"Then you are a cattle-thief yourself!" yelled Haught. "The biggest thief of all. And you are teaching these stock detectives, who were hired for that purpose, to run off my cows by the thousand."

"They are engaged," corrected Hightower, "by the Cattlemen's Association, to return all stolen cattle in their brands, and I am sure these gentlemen who are riding behind me —"

"Gentlemen!" raged Haught.

"Yes, gentlemen!" returned a detective, riding out of the line and jumping his horse against the Colonel's mount. "And if you think for a minute —"

188

"Let him go, Lee," spoke up Hightower bitterly. "By rights I ought to kill him, myself. But I promised my wife before I left home —"

"All right, then," came back Lee, "if that's the way you feel about it. But I haven't got any wife."

"These gentlemen, Mr. Haught," went on Captain Hightower, "are not accustomed to being called thieves, or to hearing me called a thief, so —"

"You'd better turn back, Colonel Haught," suggested Lee, "before we have another funeral in these parts. Red Ryan was a cow-thief and he never denied it, but —"

"Let him go, Lee," said the Captain, wearily. "Let him go."

"I'd take my oath," said Captain Hightower, "that Beau McCutcheon would never steal a cow. He's a man of sound principles, brought up by a good father, who was a sergeant in the Texas Rangers. But just to try him out, boys, I'm not going to say a word about those forty-two mavericks Haught spoke of. Beau has done good work in lining up that jury, and I spoke to him about the mavericks, myself; but the principal thing is to get these cows branded, so they won't be such a temptation. Because, with beef cattle up to twenty dollars a head and mavericks running everywhere it's almost impossible to hire a man and expect him to stay honest.

"I sincerely believe that the only way in the world to stop this rustling is to get every maverick branded. Any kind of a brand, to have something to work on. Then you boys will all lose your jobs. You'll all settle down, get a little bunch of cattle of your own, and in no time you'll be rated rich cattlemen. And now that you're young and full of blood you might as well work for me. You're paid by the Association to round up these stolen cattle, but any time you see a place like Beau's here, with good water, lots of grass and wild cattle, just ask for your time and I'll get another man. And I hope we'll always be friends.

"But when a man like Colonel Haught — no matter how wealthy he is, is always complaining about thieves, there's something the matter with him, somewhere. I've got JA cattle from the Panhandle of Texas to as far west as Tombstone, Arizona, and you boys won't get the half of them. Losing cows all the time, but at the same time I'm making money. You've got to expect a loss — and I do — but there's one thing I cannot stomach. To have a man call me a thief. Just to call off our feud I begged Colonel Haught's pardon, and what does the damned fool do? Begins all over again, complaining about Beau McCutcheon, calling the Cattlemen's Association thieves. And right there in his own back yard he has Red Ryan hiding out — the biggest cow-thief of all.

"Well, Pat Garrett killed him and now we're starting all over again to round up the whole western range, saving thousands of dollars for every honest cattleman; but sure as hell Henry Haught will buck us and do us all the dirt he can. He's a kicker, a fighter, a man that will kill eighteen neighbors for stealing, where one or two would do just as well. I don't blame him for that, because I hate a thief; but — well, here comes my boy, Beau McCutcheon!"

CHAPTER
TWENTY-EIGHT

"Thieves!"

"Nice place," observed Lee Hall, as he looked over Johnson's Spring and saw the cattle filing in to drink. "How'd you come to get it, Beau?"

"Well," admitted McCutcheon, "the man that was here before me —"

"Got killed by the Apaches," grinned Miles. "And now there's three men, waiting around on the peaks —"

"Oh, they're all right," said Beau sarcastically. "Just hiding out, for fear the Rangers will get them. Or maybe the Sheriff of Lincoln."

"But since Garrett beat Red Ryan to it," ended Miles, "w'y, all of a sudden, they're gone."

"Don't be too sure of that," warned Hightower. "They're working for Henry Haught. And I'll tell you right now, Mr. McCutcheon, you want to look out for that man. It's all right to feed these boys, when they're on the dodge, but five hundred dollars is a big reward —"

"And they never come down," said Miles. "Except at night, when a man can't see them —"

"But I know their tracks," defended Beau.

"Yes, but think of that reward, for the arrest and conviction of any man stealing a Haught cow. I'll bet," went on Miles, "I could take my Fugitive List and arrest every one of them, for something they did back in Texas."

"They're just young," qualified Hightower. "And I don't mind a cow or two as long as their heart is good. But, now that Red Ryan is dead we've got to turn over a new page. Ryan died broke, without a dime in his pocket, and he always would be broke. It was men like Butch Hardigan that got the money; and by the way, boys, we'll have to bear down on him. When he broke out of jail he moved to Arizona and started in, worse than ever. It's these renegade cattle buyers that are doing all the damage, and I'm going to stamp them out. But come over here, Mr. McCutcheon, and, while the boys are feeding their horses, I'll ask for a little report.

"I see you've got your house fixed up," he went on, kindly, "as if somebody really lived here. You weren't thinking of getting married, were you?"

"Not right away," blushed Beau. "But Musette is still waiting for me, I hope."

" 'Musette,' " repeated the Captain. "Is that the little girl you were sparking, down at Deep Lake? Well, I'm sorry to say you're in for a lot of trouble, because Henry Haught is against you. But she was a right pretty little girl — and a good one, I know. Did she give you the seeds for these hollyhocks you've got planted?"

"Well — maybe," admitted McCutcheon. "A Mexican brought them over and of course I planted them. That was early in the spring."

192

"They look fine," commented Hightower, "and I hope you can get married; but I hear Haught has warned you away."

"Yes," said Beau, "and I haven't been near her for a year. Because Ash has threatened to kill me, and I wouldn't want to kill *him*. So all I can do is watch her through these glasses; and Mr. Hightower she looks fine! If I can just get that girl —"

"You'll have to steal her, then," advised the Captain, "and maybe skip out of the country. But that's not as bad as it sounds, because then you'll get away from her people. A miserable lot of clannish Southerners —"

"Oh, I don't know," defended McCutcheon, weakly. "Gram's all right. She helps me."

"Then you'll have to steal *her*, too," nodded Hightower. "And if you don't know where to go, I'm up on the Palo Duro. We'd be mighty glad to see you and I can guarantee you a very good job. You have done very well in handling that jury and getting them to convict — when the man was guilty, of course. But this country is growing up. They don't think it's a joke to steal a man's horse now — I beg your pardon, just a slip of the tongue — and the sheriff is our friend. I can see that. But what's this fence that you've built down below here? Henry Haught was kicking about that."

"He kicks about everything," answered Beau, gloomily. "When he found that his cattle were drinking at my spring he asked why I didn't build a fence. And when I built the fence —"

193

"Yes, I know," replied the Captain. "I've seen a thousand men just like him. How do you get along with the sheriff?"

"Fine!" answered Beau, brightening up. "And by the way —" He reached into his pocket. "I sold him forty-two mavericks last week at ten dollars a head and —"

"Isn't that a rather small price?" barked Hightower. "They're fifteen or twenty dollars at Deep Lake."

"I know," acknowledged McCutcheon. "But Don Manuel is my friend. And when Hockaday rode in and drove off every cow he had that had a Texas brand on it — well, the Mexicans didn't like it."

"Those cattle were stolen, every one of them!" scolded the Captain. "Did he complain? In any way?"

"Not a word," answered Beau. "He took it like a gentleman. But of course the *comancheros* —"

"Made a business of stealing our cattle and selling them to the Mexicans."

"Yes, I know," admitted McCutcheon. "But when he rode up here and wanted to buy some more, to take the place of those that were gone —"

"You sold them for ten dollars!" accused Hightower.

"Yes, and here's the money," said Beau, handing over a roll of bills. "They were mavericks in the first place —"

"Mr. McCutcheon," blazed forth the Captain. "You're spoiling these Mexicans, I can see that. Now what do you want me to do with this?"

"Whatever you want to," answered Beau. "I reckon a Mexican has got some rights in this country as well as a

194

lot of Texans — and Red Ryan stole them back the next week."

"Well, yes," shrugged Hightower. "It was dog-eat-dog there, for a while. But just to show Don Manuel that I know how he feels, I'm going to give his money right back. On a big job like this there's bound to be some injustice and —" He thrust the money into his pocket.

"This is a hard game, McCutcheon," he said at last. "And next time I see Henry Haught I'm going to tell him what I think of him. He said you were going to *keep* this money, and make both of us out cow-thieves."

CHAPTER
TWENTY-NINE

"If a Man's Heart
Is Good"

They were off at dawn — Captain Hightower and his eight trusted men — Pat Garrett and Rye Miles. And still they were sticking to their story.

"Right in the ribs," murmured Lee Hall, slyly.

"It all happened by accident," observed another.

"They thought he was a Mexican," said a third. "Coming out to get a chunk of meat. He run right into Rye — Beau didn't even get up. Then Red entered the sleeping room — backwards — and Pat done his duty, as an officer."

"Well, have it your own way," shrugged Garrett. "I'm only telling you the truth."

"And Miles got his spurs tangled up in the plank sidewalk, so *he* couldn't get up, either. Pat had set down on his pistol, right when he needed it most —"

"Say, will you please go to hell?" inquired Garrett. "I know it sounds fishy —"

"It does," responded another Ranger, promptly.

"But if it wasn't for these accidents," observed an old-timer, wisely, "we wouldn't any of us be here now. So put me down, for one, *I believe him!*"

"So do I!" agreed Captain Hightower. "I've had stranger things happen to me. But now that we're going down to Las Cruces I want you to be nice to Manuel Duran. He has suffered some losses and took them like a gentleman, so if he's got any cows, please leave them. Butch Hardigan is the man we're looking for and he's in Tombstone, Arizona. And speaking of Duran, I want to tell you something — about our little friend and horse-thief, Beau McCutcheon."

He glanced at Rye Miles, who was still riding Hot Foot, and went on with his tale.

"If a man's heart is good," he said, "I'll trust him anywhere. With anything. You heard what Henry Haught said yesterday, about those forty-two mavericks that Beau sold to Duran for ten dollars a head? Without a word from me he reached down in his pocket and handed over — four hundred and twenty dollars! Said Don Manuel had lost all his cattle when Hockaday rode down and took them, and he wanted to pay him back. Nothing but a bunch of mavericks, anyway —"

"Good enough!" laughed the stock detectives; and — back at Johnson's Spring — Beau McCutcheon was laughing, too.

They were all gone — the Captain, the detectives, Pat Garrett and Miles, and the three men who had hid on the peak. Who they were he did not know — he never had seen them — but Pat Garrett had looked for their tracks. And, after Hightower's warning, Beau was glad to see them gone. It argued a certain lack of confidence in the man whose beef they were eating; and Beau had been sleeping out for some time, for fear they would kill him in his sleep. But now they were all gone and, leaving his gates wide open, he galloped off down the trail.

Since Red Ryan had been killed, the Haught women had been riding out again and racing across the level sands. They were out in the open, nobody could get near them, and Beau had worn a pathway to his lookout place on the cliff.

She knew he was there now, knew he was watching for her, and when the others turned back, Musette and Gram rode out boldly to where he could see her buckskin suit. The trim white jacket, the buckskin leggings, the skirt that came to her knees; and when she got close enough, behind a drifted sandhill, she stopped short and rode in circles.

It was the Indian sign for "Danger ahead" as well as "Come to me!" And without thinking twice Beau loped down the trail and galloped out to meet them. She was the same, only taller, and old Tla's wife had made her an Indian saddle — high in the pommel, higher yet in the cantle, with long-fringed saddlebags on both sides — and she rode out to meet him, laughing.

"Just for a minute," she called. "I knew you were up there, watching. And Gram has come down, to make the suit all prim and proper, but I just *had* to show you my dress. Old Tla was so pleased he offered to marry me, but he's got two wives, already."

"Yes, yes," answered Beau. "It's the custom of the country, with the Apaches. And with your hair down in front —"

"Like an Indian!" she shouted. "Oh, Beau, have you been watching all the time?"

"Watching and waiting," he said. "And now, do I get a kiss?"

"Why not?" she asked. "We're still engaged, aren't we? And give Gram a kiss, too! Because if it wasn't for her —"

Gram cantered up sedately, in a black velvet riding suit, and he kissed her, horse to horse.

"Young man," she warned. "I shouldn't have done this, and we'll have to go right back. But now that we're free from the terror of that man that was watching us —"

"We can ride again!" broke in Musette. "Isn't this grand?"

She spread out her buckskin skirt, all decorated with beads and fringes, and he handed her over a book.

"It's *The Merchant of Venice*," he said. "I hope you like it."

"Oh, I'll keep it with my other book!" she responded. "My precious little *Romeo and Juliet*. Have you got any more? Oh, Beau!"

"Not *with* me," he said. "But next time I come down —"

"We must go now," decided Gram.

"When you want me, just ride in circles!" directed Beau.

"I want you all the time," she countered, smiling; and her grandmother dragged her away.

"Well, well," murmured McCutcheon, as he watched them gallop off. "And it all happened so quick, like that. But I wonder. I wonder where their men-folks are. I'd better get back to camp."

There was something wrong, Beau could see that at a glance as his horse labored up the steep canyon. The strong gate he had built had been knocked down, it lay in the dust on its hinges; and out among the rocks, bruised and crumpled and bleeding, was a huge man who was gasping for air. He was a repulsive-looking creature, with half the clothes torn off of him and a month's growth of beard on his jaw. Yet, though he seemed to hear McCutcheon he kept his eyes shut, cursing feebly with every breath.

From the tracks in the dirt he had fallen off his horse, crashing through the gate as he fell; and Beau straightened out his head thinking at first he had broken his neck.

"Uhhr!" grunted the stranger. "Git me out of here, mister — and give me something to eat. I ain't bad hurt — been four days without grub. Has that long-legged sheriff gone away?"

Then Beau knew who he was — one of the three men hiding out from Pat Garrett. They had been out in the hills for four days.

"Get up on my horse," directed McCutcheon, "and I'll pack you up to the spring."

200

He laid hold of the huge form and boosted it into the saddle, and still the stranger kept his eyes shut. But he held his place, and, ahead of them as they climbed, ran a bunch of Henry Haught's cows. They had been waiting, as always, to get through the fence and sup the sweet water of Johnson's Spring. Below them, on the desert, it was all alkali and gypsum, and they rushed on clear up to the corral.

"Put me down!" wailed the man, half falling from the saddle, "and give me something to eat. I don't care what it is, but I've got —"

He lopped over and fell — a mighty burden — and McCutcheon dragged him into the house. But, when Beau looked around, the room was bare. His entire food supply was gone.

"Kill me one of those yearlings," begged the stranger, rousing up, "and give me his liver to eat. Or the sweetbread — or the guts. I'm dying."

Out of a litter of smashed glass Beau snatched up his carbine and hurried down to the spring. The cattle stood there in bunches so full of water they could hardly stir; but every one of them was branded HH. McCutcheon rushed in among them, picked out a yearling and laid him low the first shot. Then he cut out the liver and sweetbread and hurried back to the house.

"Never mind a fire," grunted the man as he dipped the sweetbread in the ashes and ate it raw. "Now git me the ribs and I'll show you some eating. Jest putt them over the coals."

201

"You must be from West Virginia," said Beau, "the way you pronounced that 'putt.'" And the stranger opened his eyes.

Then McCutcheon saw why he had kept his eyes closed. In the pupil of one eye there was a round, red spot. He sighed deeply and closed them again.

"Don't turn me over to the Rangers!" he begged. "Or are you a Ranger, yourself?"

"No, I'm not," answered Beau, "but my pardner is, and someone has been robbing my house. They've smashed all my windows and —"

"Did they steal all your grub?" asked the man.

"Every bit of it," answered McCutcheon, after a search.

"Well, never mind, I won't stay long. Jest give me lots of beef and —"

He turned over and went to sleep.

202

CHAPTER
THIRTY

Hobo Tracks

He was still fast asleep when Rye Miles came back from Las Cruces and looked him over suspiciously.

"What's *he* doing here?" he demanded; and still the man did not look up.

"I found him down at the gate," explained Beau. "His horse had bucked him off. And when I packed him back home all my cows were gone, and every bit of our grub."

"Never mind about the grub," soothed Miles. "I brought some more out from town. But who is this yahoo? Is he dead, or what? And why doesn't he open his eyes?"

"Search me," answered Beau. "That's just the way I found him, and we can't let him lay there and die."

"You keep on taking in these hobos," observed Rye, "and you'll get lousy, to say the least. Look at that pair of *tewas* he's wearing over his boots — rawhide, with the hair worn off."

"*I* know!" said McCutcheon. "He's that man with the moccasins that's been watching our camp from the peak. But his horse nearly killed him and ran away, so we'll have to keep him a while."

"Keep him if you want to," replied Miles. "I've got to go over to Lincoln. Pat made me a deputy, to run down those cow-thieves, and I'll bet you a dollar he's one of them. Hey, you!" he shouted; and the man woke up with a start.

"Putting it on," commented Rye. "No man can sleep like that. He was listening, all the time."

"No I wasn't!" protested the hobo. "I'm jest down on my luck. Horse bucked me off — I'll have to walk to town."

"Well, let him stay," decided Miles at last; and in the morning he was gone.

Half the beef was gone, too; and though they did not notice it, it was the half that bore the brand.

He was the last of the hobos, hiding out from the officers and living on McCutcheon's beef, and Beau went about repairing the damage. There was the gate to be mended and, when he went down to fix it, he saw the hobo's tracks, where he pulled out without saying good-by; but when he brought out his glasses and looked for Musette he saw her riding wildly.

She had been riding circles half a day, while he was mending the gate in the canyon, and when he galloped down she was crying.

"Oh, Beau!" she sobbed. "He got away. That man you thought was dying. He just put it on, to get you to kill one of our cattle and now he's gone into Las Cruces, to swear out a warrant against you. And he had the calf-skin with him, wrapped up and labeled Exhibit A."

"Trapped!" shrugged Beau. "I knew he was trying to catch me. It was to get that Five Hundred Dollars Reward."

"They just laughed at us," wept Gram. "My own son turned against me. He's doing it to hurt Captain Hightower. And now you've got to go, before they come and arrest you; and you'll never see Musette again."

"Not right here," admitted McCutcheon. "But this is New Mexico, Gram, and I've got a job waiting in Texas. Captain Hightower will take care of me — he won't let them extradite me. And I'll come back for you, Musette."

"Oh, they're all set against you," wailed Musette. "For what you did to Ash. And father has promised this stock detective five hundred dollars more, if he makes it stick."

" 'Detective'!" repeated Beau. "That man I've been feeding?"

"He makes a business of going around and catching cow-thieves, and they let you come down here on purpose. So father and Ash could drive off your cattle and plant some more of their own. Then he starved himself — on purpose — and got thrown off his horse so you'd help him. So you'd kill him a beef."

"Well, I did," acknowledged McCutcheon. "The man was starving. But there's nothing wrong about that."

"You'll see!" warned Gram. "They've all gone to Las Cruces, to swear out a warrant against you. Henry and Ash and this terrible Hargis — he's one of those West Virginia Hargisses."

"My God!" exclaimed Beau. "The feudists?"

"The same," nodded Gram. "And you'd better get out of here —"

"Oh, I don't know," shrugged McCutcheon. "I happen to know Duran, the sheriff. And Garrett. You can't run a man in, when he hasn't done wrong. Rye Miles came home last night, and Pat saw him."

"Then you'd better see Miles, jest as soon as you can," said Gram. "You'd better see him, anyway. Because this flat out here is in Doña Ana County and our fort is in Lincoln, across the line. They can't arrest a man there for what he did in Doña Ana."

"No, I know they can't," answered Beau. "But if I skip out over there, or go back into Texas, that makes me a fugitive from justice."

"That's better than being sent to prison," argued Gram. "And you're branded a convict for life."

"All the same," stated McCutcheon, "I won't run away. And — here's the old lady coming."

He jerked his thumb towards a woman galloping out to them, and Musette leaned against him and cried.

"Oh, I just hate her," she moaned. "My own mother!"

"You leave her to me," spoke up Gram. "That woman has ruined my son. He was jest as good and kind — and then she got hold of him and made him a regular devil."

"And Ash, too," added Beau. "I'll have to kill him yet."

"No, you stay here," commanded Gram. She set off at a gallop, her long riding-skirt slatting in the wind, and McCutcheon glanced at Musette.

"I had our house all ready," he mourned. "I was going to ask you to marry me. But now that this has come up — can you wait for me a while, Musette?"

"I *will* wait for you," promised Musette. "I don't care what they say! And then we'll go away, where nobody will know us, and —"

"No!" he said. "You can't marry an ex-convict! The name will follow us all our lives. But wait until after the trial. And then —"

"I'll wait," promised Musette; and kissed him.

They watched Mrs. Haught as she galloped up — a little woman, thin-faced and vindictive — and Musette heaved a great sigh.

"You Musette!" yapped her mother. "Didn't you hear what I told you? I said: *Leave this man alone!* He's been following you around —"

"He has not!" denied Gram.

"Well, he's been giving her books — and such vile, vulgar books — I took the last one away from her. And it was all about a woman who put on men's clothes —"

"I don't care!" answered Musette. "You never read your Bible — and I think it's a *beautiful* book!"

"You come with me," ordered her mother sternly. "Have you told him about Duane? Well, if Mr. McCutcheon was a gentleman, he'd understand. My daughter," she went on, dragging her forward, "is engaged to marry a young man of very excellent family."

"I am not," contradicted Musette.

"Just as good as engaged," corrected Mrs. Haught. "He's just waiting for her to grow up."

"I'm grown up, already," replied Musette, with spirit. "And I'll let you know that I am over sixteen, and can marry whoever I will. And one thing I'll say — I'll never marry Duane."

"You are a very disobedient daughter," scolded her mother; and Gram motioned them into a gallop.

"Here comes my son," she said. "And we might as well get across this line, before he has you arrested. And please don't shoot Ash — he's very impetuous — and his mother has made him into a perfect fool. I declare, since the day Henry married her —"

Musette broke away from her mother and took Beau's hand in hers.

"I love you, Beau," she said. "And I'll always wait for you. Is that all right? Then good-by."

She rode away with Gram without looking back, and Haught and Ash thundered up.

"Oh, here you are!" scoffed Haught, as McCutcheon kept on his way. "I've just sworn out a warrant to have you arrested for stealing one of my cows. But if you'll ride across that line and keep a-going —"

"I won't promise that," said Beau. "If you've got any papers, go ahead and serve them. I'm going over to Lincoln."

"Just as well," shrugged Haught. "I can have them served there. If, of course, you don't change your mind when you see the evidence I've got."

"I won't," replied McCutcheon. "Where's your friend, Mr. Hargis?"

"He's gone away, to hide in the hills, until the day of the trial; and not all your friends — not Jack Hightower himself — can keep you from going to the Pen."

"So you say," answered Beau. "But there's a judge and a jury who will have the say about that."

"Can they get around the law? Can they get around the evidence? I have the hide of a yearling calf, killed by you in your corral, and a witness to prove that he saw it. As for my daughter, Mr. McCutcheon, she is a very headstrong girl; but I think, with your permission, I'd rather not have any horse-thieves in our family."

"Very well, sir," said McCutcheon, turning red. "Is that all? Then with your permission I'll ride over to Lincoln and consult with Mr. Miles about this."

"Miles!" yelled Haught. "That presumptuous rascal? Well, I think, next to a horse-thief, I'd draw the line at a sergeant in the Texas Rangers."

"Is that a message?" inquired Beau.

"It is!" raged Haught. "It is!"

CHAPTER
THIRTY-ONE

The Sheriff of Lincoln

A great change had come over Rye Miles since Beau had seen him the day before. He was smoking cigars in the Sheriff's office and looking over some papers, and now he had that officer-look. Hot Foot was down below, eating rolled barley instead of corn, and he whickered as McCutcheon went past. But Beau did not speak to him or stop to rub his nose. His master did not like it. Since the day Miles had come out to Johnson's Canyon, Rye had had his reservations; for he never could forget that Beau had once stolen his horse. Next to murder, that was the unforgivable sin.

"Hello!" he said, in his big, booming voice, shoving his hat further back on his head. "Mr. McCutcheon, I believe. How's everything, Beau? You made a quick trip. Did that hobo die on you, or what?"

"He skipped out on me," complained Beau. "And say, did you notice? That yearling had an HH brand on it."

"The hell!" exclaimed Miles, incredulously, grabbing a paper and making a note.

"Anything else?" he asked.

"He took it down to the fort and gave it to Henry Haught, and by the time I got there they'd gone over to Las Cruces and sworn out an information. Stealing an HH calf."

"Bad!" commented Rye, still writing. "Was that man a cattle detective?"

"Certainly was. A Hargis, from West Virginia. He's hiding out till October first, when court is called. Do you reckon you can find him, Miles?"

"Sure thing," answered Rye, confidently. "That's my business now. I'm sheriff. Pat went along with the Chief to Tombstone, and you know who's running this country. John Hightower, by grab. All he expects is results, and Pat Garrett let Red Ryan escape. You've got to be good, to hold *this* job."

"Well, you're good, all right," beamed Beau. "But I never looked for anything like that."

"Ketching Red Ryan was what did it," nodded Rye, portentously. "And remember — don't say a word about that story we made up. Now what can I do for you, Beau?"

"Catch Hargis," answered McCutcheon; and smiled.

"I'll do that," promised Miles. "In twenty-four hours. But I haven't got a jail that will hold him. That man is a criminal, I could tell by his eyes. Did you notice that spot of red?"

"In the left eye," said Beau. "And he always looked down, so nobody he talked to would see it. A big, hulking fellow, starved down so I'd think he was hungry. He told me he was hiding out from Pat."

211

"He was, too," grunted Rye. "A desperate character. Who juggled those cattle around?"

"Henry Haught and Ash. While I was down seeing Musette. They had it all framed up."

"And now what?" inquired the sheriff. "What does Haught want?"

"To disgrace Captain Hightower, by showing me up for a thief. Tried to drift me out of the country."

"Aha!" exclaimed Rye. "So that's his racket! Well, you stay right here. Don't you move. What color was Hargis' hair?"

"Sandy. With a month's growth of beard. Wearing *tewas* — his boots were wore out. No coat at all — went around in his undershirt. But that eye of his gave him away. He never looked up, until I heard him say 'putt' instead of put. I asked him then if he was from West Virginia — where those mountaineers live, you know — and his eyes bugged out like a rabbit's. Then I saw that spot. It was red."

"Just a moment!" exclaimed Miles, reaching over for a pamphlet; and he ran through a dozen pages. "'Nelson Hargis,'" he read. "'Wanted for stealing a roan horse, fifteen hands high, a pacer. Large man, rough-looking, sandy hair and beard. Frequently seen in dance halls and saloons. Red spot in left eye. $50 reward. Wire or write Jeff Adams, Sheriff, Hereford, Deafsmith County.' Does that give you an idea, Mr. McCutcheon?"

Beau smiled and nodded his head.

"Fugitive List," explained Rye. "They send 'em out to all us Rangers. I thought I remembered that eye.

212

How's everything down at the Fort? Didn't happen to see Odette?"

"Not a chance. Barney Hoops was watching me. But the old man sent you a message. Said he'd rather not have any horse-thieves in his family; and, next to a horse-thief —"

"As long as you live," shrugged Miles, "that's always going to be against you. I never said anything, Beau; but when you stole Hot Foot and headed for New Mexico —"

"Next to a horse-thief," went on McCutcheon, "he said he barred Texas Rangers."

"What?" yelled Rye, leaping up. "He sent that message to me?"

"I wouldn't have told you," began Beau. "Only —"

"Well, damn his hide," cursed Miles. "The murdering bastard! Hanging eighteen men with their horse-hobbles! You tell him — no, wait. You tell him from me — if Odette wasn't the prettiest woman in the world I'd — I'd never think of marrying into his family. You tell him that now and — no, I take it all back, McCutcheon. A girl ain't responsible for the acts of her father, but if I don't make Henry Haught feel sorry he spoke, my name is Sickum and I'm a dog. The first thing I do is count all Haught's cattle and increase his taxes two hundred per cent. And sure as hell I'm going to mention that Brazos killing, and how the Rangers were hunting him everywhere. Until the Chief told 'em he'd looked into that hanging and every damn one of them deserved it."

"But he told me," added Beau, "Haught never needed to hang more than one or two."

"Well, with all that behind him," cursed Rye, "he'd better be careful what he says. And this idea of having you arrested — it's all done to spite the Chief. We're going to have a clean-up in this county that will make every cow-thief hunt his hole. The biggest thief of all — a man who stole his thousands — is sleeping in my jail, right now; and it wouldn't hold a cat. Yes, sir, Martin Hockaday, the man that ruled the Pecos and ran sixty thousand head of cows! But he would steal cattle — the lawyers got hold of him — and he's been living around in jails for a year. More judgments against him than would pack hell a mile, and still he won't come through. He could pay them all off in twenty-four hours but he won't do it. He says it's *wrong*."

The new sheriff laughed raucously and began to run through his papers.

"Go down and see him, Beau," he said, "while I look over this mail. If there's anything I hate it's paper work, and Pat has been away for a month. Then we'll go down together and find where this Hargis went, and make him hard to ketch. Haught must've given him some money to eat on — he's been starving himself for four days — and we'll show Mr. Haught what the Rangers can do when they really take after a man. W'y, Beau, the Chief would never forgive me if I left Hargis loose twenty-four hours. And you! All the Captain can talk about is how goodhearted and *honest* you are. You'll find Exhibit A sitting out in front of the hotel and telling stories to make the boys laugh. And still insisting it's *wrong*."

He laughed again, consumedly, while he shuffled through the letters and McCutcheon went down the stairs. The same back stairs that Deputy Bell had painted red with his life's blood when Ryan hit him on the run. The same set of stairs that Bob Ollinger had descended, just before Red shot him through the heart. And here was Martin Hockaday, sleeping out in the jail because the court decision was *unjust*.

CHAPTER
THIRTY-TWO

Martin Hockaday

He was sitting on the back steps by the jail and now he was old and decrepit, though he looked up with a smile. He was haggard and broken down, without many more days to live, but he recognized Beau at a glance.

"W'y, hello thar!" he greeted, rising up to shake hands. "I don't remember your name if I even knowed it, but you're the cowboy that broke out of the Fort Davis jail and came in with his head all wropped up in a rag. The Injuns called you Bloody Head — they call you that yet when some of them come to town. You got into a fight with the Comanche Injuns when they jumped Jack's horse herd at Pope's Crossing, and Hightower saved your life. He was a great feller — Jack — so honest he leaned over backwards. And he never goes through town that he don't hunt up old Martin.

"'Martin,' he says, 'what the hell is the matter with you that you didn't pay that trifling judgment?'"

"It's only fifty thousand dollars — and costs — and all the rest of it; but I tell him: 'No! I won't pay!' There's such a thing as right and wrong in this world, and I paid every dollar I owed. Then I come into this country and became the King of the Pecos, with sixty thousand head of cattle at one time; and those men I'd gone in with — it was a meat-packing enterprise — by Ned, they went broke *again*. This was way up in Round Rock, on the borders of Kansas, and I never heard a word about it; until this big lawyer, with a face like a meat-ax, came around and levied an attachment on every dollar I had." He laughed again, brokenly, and Beau sat down in the sun.

"Yes, sir," sighed Hockaday. "I could have settled up at that time for fifty-eight thousand dollars, and I had it right in my safe. The famous Salamander Safe you hear about — but I said no, it wasn't right. I'd paid my full share of that first bankruptcy case and it left me practically strapped. A lawyer told me later that all I had to do was put a notice in the paper that I wasn't responsible for any further debts of the company and they couldn't collect a cent, but what did I know about that? I'd never been to school, more than a common education — and I just hate these lawyer fellers."

He stuffed his corncob pipe with Star Plug tobacco and scratched a match on his pants.

"If they ever get hold of a man," he went on, "that's lived a decent, honest life, they'll strip him to his last dollar and shut him up in jail for life. I sleep in that jail thar — and I will, all my life, before I'll pay this unjust fine — and all the time I've got thousands of cattle, still rambling over the Pecos Plains. But this lawyer, by Ned, got hold of me; and for seven months, while the Lincoln war was going on and they stealing everything I had, he shut me up in the Las Vegas jail.

217

"Seven months, before he would believe that I wouldn't pay. Nothing to eat but beans and tortillas, twice a day — and then, when he turned me loose, he began a civil suit. For defamation of the character, mind you, of Michael O'Grady, the Lord of Lincoln County and the damnedest cow-thief in the world. A hundred thousand dollars he wanted for my saying publicly that Mike O'Grady was a thief, and when I failed to appear in court the judge give him the whole wad, by default. Then this lawyer, whose name I don't even dare to mention for fear he'll sue me again, wrote back to the company that had gone into bankruptcy and got judgments for two hundred thousand more. Or maybe it was three hundred thousand — I never intended to pay — so here I lay, at the mercy of the courts, and all my property gone.

"My friend, Captain Hightower, never goes through here that he don't stop and beg me to pay. He says that in six months he can pay the judgments off — then he cusses and goes away. He's a fine man, Jack Hightower, and honest as the day is long. We were pardners in the old days, and he never cut back a cow. Then my nephews stole some cattle, which they had no right to do — only the Comanches had stole their whole herd — and Jack said he was sorry, we'd always been friends — but he'd never buy cattle from a thief.

"'A *thief*,' he called me, "and I laughed at the time; but from that moment my troubles began. Red Ryan came in — a fine, active boy with no more fear than a rattlesnake — and when he quit he took my whole herd with him. Or half of them — he left the rest. Said he

218

just wanted to see if that lawyer was any good. I'd hired one to straighten out my affairs. And inside of a month that lawyer was dead. The O'Grady crowd had killed him.

"Well, so it goes," he sighed. "And nobody ever comes to see me any more. Except Captain Hightower and these Mescalero Apaches who used to steal every horse I had. Now they still come around and shake hands with me. What are you doing now — er, Bloody Head? That was a great fight you put up when the Comanches attacked you, and Jack Hightower never forgot it.

"'That boy's a true Texan,' he said. 'He'd make a damned good Ranger.' And this Ranger we've got now, in place of Pat Garrett, is another one of the same kind. Jack was always hiring Rangers — and here comes one, now!" he laughed, as Rye Miles came bouncing down the stairs. "How's everything, Rye? Going away?"

"Back in twenty-four hours," answered Miles. "But you don't need to tell 'em I'm gone. Just make yourself to home, up in my office, and tell the cook to feed you good. Only prisoner I've got, Mr. Hockaday. Got to treat you right or you might get mad and run away."

He beckoned Beau to follow him with a jerk of the head, and passed him the Fugitive List.

"Found a good description of Barney Hoops," he said. "Good enough for my purpose, anyway. He'll be a fugitive, before I get through with him. I don't like that yap, at all."

He swung up on Hot Foot and galloped away, and two hours later he pulled up at a roadhouse, where they dismounted and ordered a drink.

"Evening, Joe," he said. "Meet my friend, Mr. McCutcheon."

"Oh, *Mister* McCutcheon," grinned the barkeep, shaking hands; and he set out two drinks more. "That was a pretty slick play you boys pulled off, when you got Red Ryan last week."

"Only an accident," answered Rye Miles, dryly. "Say, who's been going by here? I'm sheriff now and we're out on a scout. Seen any suspicious characters?"

"One!" reported Joe, pouring out another drink and holding up his glass. "I know, one drink's your limit, Mister Miles, but I wish you every success. Won't you join me, Mister McCutcheon? So you're looking for a suspicious character? Well, he went up the road toward White Oaks, not more than two hours ago, and he wouldn't even stop for a drink. Riding a big, roan horse, stripped down to his undershirt, and looked like he'd been through the war."

"Anything else?" inquired Rye Miles, negligently. "I knew if I came by here you'd be watching the trail. What kind of shoes did he wear?"

"An old pair of boots, with rawhide *tewas*. I noticed them in particular."

"See his eyes?" asked Rye; and the saloon-keeper shook his head.

"Must've been in a fight — both eyes were half closed — and he never even looked up."

"I'll have to look him over," observed Miles. "How's everything with you, Mr. Allen? Well, much obliged for taking notice of this. A big, hulking feller, huh?"

He swung up on Hot Foot and winked back at Beau as they thundered off up the road.

"Speedy work," he commented. "He's gone to hide up there somewhere. A dead mining camp — Johnny Seide will know."

Johnny Seide was out waiting for them as they stepped off at the door and ordered a couple of drinks.

"How's everything?" inquired Miles. "Mines opened up yet? Shake hands with Mr. McCutcheon — an old friend of Captain Hightower."

"This is on the house!" grinned Seide. "I heard all about you, Mr. McCutcheon. Captain Hightower done the community a real service when he brought you boys in here, to stop this stealing. Red Ryan is on my books for over eighty dollars, which I never expected he'd pay. But say, boys, wasn't there something mysterious about the way you come up on Red? Twelve o'clock at night, and running around in his socks!"

"Pat done it," answered Miles. "It was all an accident. He went in the house to get some information —"

"Like hell," observed Johnny Seide.

"Well, what's going on?" asked Rye. "Seen any suspicious characters go by?"

"One," said Johnny, "and he was a dandy. Had rawhide *tewas* over his boots, like he'd been prospecting, up in the hills."

"What kind of a horse was he riding? A big roan, kind of snorty?"

"He was run down to a shadder," reported Seide. "And here's another clue you might use. He never looked up, even when he tossed off two drinks, and —"

"Where did he go?" demanded Rye Miles, eagerly. "You ought to be a detective, Johnny."

"Well, I do keep my eyes open," acknowledged Seide. "Part of my business, you know. He went up that wash to that old deserted tunnel, and I haven't seen him since. Kind of a hobo camp up there where the water runs out —"

"He's my meat!" exclaimed Rye. "Come on."

He hammered off up the wash as if his life depended on it, but around the first turn he stopped short.

"Let me do this," he directed, "and I'll show you how the Rangers work. We won't jump him out — I want some information first. But if he starts to git ugly keep out of the way and I'll show you something good. This man is a bad hombre — very likely a killer — And the thing is to git him to surrender. So we'll kid him along until I snap on the handcuffs. Then I'll bear down on him, Beau. I know damned well who put him up to this, and I want him to come clean. About Henry Haught and the rest. After that I'll take him over to the Texas line, where Eem Cole is stationed now, and he'll arrest him for stealing that roan horse. Then the sheriff of Deafsmith County will pay that fifty dollars reward and I'll divide up with Eem — if he don't let him git away! After that, Mr. McCutcheon, we don't need to worry about Hargis turning up in court — to swear you into jail. But don't kill him — unless you have to. It looks kind of bad on the books."

He put spurs to Hot Foot, who was off with a rush, and when they dashed around the corner, here was Mr. Hargis, unarmed.

"Hello, there!" shouted Miles in his big, booming voice, stopping well away from his man. "I'm the sheriff of Lincoln County; and you know this hombre, I reckon. He's the man whose camp you've been robbing when you were working for Henry Haught, and don't try to tell me any different."

Hargis's face turned a ghastly white, and he stepped away from the fire; but when he saw McCutcheon, looking mildly on, he straightened up and smiled. A wry, crooked smile — and he relaxed.

"Yes, sir," he said. "If it's any of your business, I did eat this cowboy's grub. But what is that to you, Mister Sheriff? This happened in Doña Ana County."

"Well," acknowledged Miles, "that's right, Mr. Hargis. But the saloon keeper just reported a suspicious character up here, so —"

"You came up hyar?" ended Hargis, arrogantly. "Seems to me you're taking a good deal for granted — riding into a man's camp like this. Many a man has been killed for less than that. And don't you know you're harboring a thief? That man stole a calf and I've swore out an information against him."

" 'Information,' hey," repeated Miles, insultingly. "What do you know about the law?"

"I'm a cattle detective — been at it for years — and Henry Haught employed me to watch this boy and

223

report to him when he stole his next cow. That was just yesterday — or the day before — and at last I've got the dead wood on him. Caught him in the act, and I've got the brand to prove it. Exhibit A — Nelson Hargis versus Beau McCutcheon. Grand larceny of a calf."

"Hm," murmured Miles. "'Nelson Hargis' — that sounds familiar. Any relation to the Hargis clan, of West Virginia?"

"No, sir!" denied Hargis. "I am not, sir. And what business is it of yours if I am?"

"None whatever," responded Rye, meekly. "Only I happened to have an old Fugitive List, that was issued to the Texas Rangers —"

"Are you a Texas Ranger?" barked Hargis.

"Well, no," admitted Miles. "But they send them out to all us officers and, somehow, that name sounds familiar. What was your father's name, Mister Hargis?"

"None of your damned business!" snapped the detective. "I'm a regularly appointed official —"

"Appointed by whom?" inquired Rye. "As sheriff of Lincoln County it is my duty, Mr. Hargis, to question all suspicious characters, and find out what they're doing here. Now what was your father's name?"

"I refuse to answer," replied Hargis, "on the ground that I might incriminate myself."

"Git that gun!" directed Miles, as Hargis lay sprawling, and Beau snatched the pistol away.

It was hid under his shirt, tucked away in his waistband, and Hargis submitted with a groan.

"What the hell are you doing?" he asked. "What charges have you got against me?"

"Resisting an officer," replied Miles. "Stick out your hands while I put on these grips. No fooling, or I'll bash you over the head. All right, then!"

He swung his heavy pistol forward and, with a wrist-movement, rapped him over the skull.

"Now put these nippers on him," directed Rye. "And hang these leg-irons on — tight."

CHAPTER
THIRTY-THREE

The Circuit Court

The Circuit Court of Doña Ana County was still in session, and Sheriff Duran led Beauregard McCutcheon to take the defendant's chair. The same old Beau who had presided over the jury, only now he was standing trial.

"Nelson Hargis versus Beauregard McCutcheon," announced the Clerk of the Court. "Is Nelson Hargis in Court?"

"Nelson Hargis!" intoned the bailiff, and glanced expectantly at Duran.

"Your Honor," responded the Prosecuting Attorney, "the complaining witness is not present."

"Case dismissed!" ruled Judge Bristol. "Defendant discharged. Court adjourned."

There was a buzz in the courtroom, where half the Haught family was assembled, and then Henry Haught jumped to his feet.

"This man —" he shouted, pointing an accusing finger at Beau —

"Order in the court!" thundered the bailiff, and Sheriff Duran led McCutcheon out.

"Now, my friend," he smiled. "We have another official duty to perform. Or is this young lady smiling at *me?* You do not require the presence of the priest. A justice of the peace will do just as well and the County Clerk will issue the license. I shall be glad to stand up with you — and perhaps this dear lady —"

He bowed to Gram, who was lingering near them, and Beau kissed her on both cheeks.

"Shall we ride up the trail?" he asked. "To our house at Johnson's Canyon?"

He picked up the little bride tenderly and swung her on the dish-faced Indian pony. Hosteen Tla's young wife fell in behind them and they went off at a gallop, up the old Jornada del Muerte, that led along the mesa.

"I want Grace Pelchu to go with us," smiled Musette. "She made my dress, you know. And Don Manuel showed us where to build our house. We can look down from the cliff and see Gram."

"I wish you every happiness," murmured Duran. "And Hosteen Tla will come by often. But here are others, close behind us. The Sheriff of Lincoln County."

"Welcome!" greeted Musette. "And dear Odette, too. But there is Papa, down on the White Sands, waiting for us."

"And Ash, too," grumbled the sheriff. "I want to see your father, right now, and tell him where he gets off."

He loped off down the trail and Odette and Gram followed, although Rye had not invited them.

"Mr. Haught, Sir!" spoke up Miles. "I want to tell you something and no beating around the bush about it. You may think you run this county, but you're talking to the Sheriff of Lincoln County. Now what would you think of paying five hundred percent increase in taxes, to support our schools and officers? All right. You'll have to do it. And another thing — as an officer —

"Your place, Mr. Haught, has become a den of thieves and criminals. In particular, Barney Hoops and Ash Haught. I don't care whose son he is. Get 'em out of Lincoln County, right now. This man Nelson Hargis was a disgrace to New Mexico. Sheriff Duran will take care of him. That is all, Sir, and kindly remember that you are talking to a man who was a Texas *Ranger*."

"Yes, sir," answered Henry Haught.

Hosteen Tla rose up and turned his fierce, glaring eyes on his woman, but not with any malice, of course. But Grace Pelchu, the pretty one, held back. It was time for them to go.

"Here! For you!" she said and handed Musette some beaded moccasins. Very pretty, with the toes turned up, to protect her feet from the thorns.

"Oh! You dear!" murmured Musette, and kissed her tawny cheeks.

Tla gave Beau a pair of rawhide hobbles and they sat down in front of their new home, where Beau could reach out and hold her hand.

"What is that?" she asked, as a bird began to trill, and McCutcheon pointed to a cedar tree where a mockingbird sang.

"It is the nightingale," he quoted, and Musette moved even closer yet.

"No, it is the lark," she said. And Grace Pelchu looked back and smiled.

ISIS publish a wide range of books in large print, from fiction to biography. Any suggestions for books you would like to see in large print or audio are always welcome. Please send to the Editorial Department at:

ISIS Publishing Limited
7 Centremead
Osney Mead
Oxford OX2 0ES

A full list of titles is available free of charge from:

Ulverscroft Large Print Books Limited

(UK)
The Green
Bradgate Road, Anstey
Leicester LE7 7FU
Tel: (0116) 236 4325

(Australia)
P.O. Box 314
St Leonards
NSW 1590
Tel: (02) 9436 2622

(USA)
P.O. Box 1230
West Seneca
N.Y. 14224-1230
Tel: (716) 674 4270

(Canada)
P.O. Box 80038
Burlington
Ontario L7L 6B1
Tel: (905) 637 8734

(New Zealand)
P.O. Box 456
Feilding
Tel: (06) 323 6828

Details of **ISIS** complete and unabridged audio books are also available from these offices. Alternatively, contact your local library for details of their collection of **ISIS** large print and unabridged audio books.